Juliet remained frozen where she stood.

She was unable to move forward or backward. A metaphor for her life?

Rob let the door fall shut behind them. "What's wrong?"

"Nothing." She sighed. "Sophie, stroke Moose gently. He likes to be petted on his head, his back and behind his ears."

Giving Juliet a tentative smile, Sophie did as instructed. Moose's tail, curled over his body, swished happily.

Rob took a breath. "Thank you."

She looked at him. "For what?"

"For giving Sophie back her smile." His voice was thick with emotion.

A lump rose in her throat. Rob joined his daughter on the couch with Moose. Her heart did a treacherous lurch. What was it about the man that affected her so?

She was afraid the more time she spent with him, the more she would… What? Enjoy his company? Have to acknowledge her loneliness?

After Josh died, she'd sworn off romantic relationships for good. And her strategy had been working great. Until she'd met Rob Melbourne again.

Lisa Carter and her family make their home in North Carolina. In addition to her Love Inspired novels, she writes romantic suspense. When she isn't writing, Lisa enjoys traveling to romantic locales, teaching writing workshops and researching her next exotic adventure. She has strong opinions on barbecue and ACC basketball. She loves to hear from readers. Connect with Lisa at lisacarterauthor.com.

Books by Lisa Carter

Love Inspired

Coast Guard Courtship
Coast Guard Sweetheart
Falling for the Single Dad
The Deputy's Perfect Match
The Bachelor's Unexpected Family
The Christmas Baby
Hometown Reunion
His Secret Daughter
The Twin Bargain
Stranded for the Holidays
The Christmas Bargain
A Chance for the Newcomer
A Safe Place for Christmas

K-9 Companions

Finding Her Way Back

Visit the Author Profile page at LoveInspired.com.

Finding Her Way Back

Lisa Carter

LOVE INSPIRED
INSPIRATIONAL ROMANCE

LOVE INSPIRED®
INSPIRATIONAL ROMANCE

ISBN-13: 978-1-335-75905-4

Finding Her Way Back

Copyright © 2022 by Lisa Carter

Recycling programs
for this product may
not exist in your area.

This edition published by arrangement with Harlequin Books S.A.

For questions and comments about the quality of this book, please contact us at CustomerService@Harlequin.com.

Love Inspired
22 Adelaide St. West, 41st Floor
Toronto, Ontario M5H 4E3, Canada
www.LoveInspired.com

Printed in U.S.A.

Now the God of hope fill you with all joy and peace in believing, that ye may abound in hope, through the power of the Holy Ghost.
—*Romans* 15:13

This book is dedicated to the memory of my late mother-in-law, Patricia Carter. You grieved much because you loved deeply. Thank you for loving us. The best things are worth the wait. And at your home-going, how joyous must have been those much-longed-for reunions. Until we meet again. Love, Lisa

Chapter One

Juliet Newkirk told herself it was absolutely ridiculous to feel so nervous about meeting Rob Melbourne again.

But sitting in her car, parked beside the curb in front of his house in Laurel Grove, she made no move to get out. From his carrier in the back seat, her dog, Moose, gave two short barks.

"I know. I know." She glanced in the rearview mirror at the little tricolor canine. "We've done this dozens of times. Just another case. He's just a new client. No big deal."

Only somehow it was.

Because of the intense media coverage surrounding the shooting last month, this wasn't any old case. A lot of important people were taking a keen interest in her involvement in this situation.

The sort of people on the grant-funding committee of the hospital board with the power to make her dream of establishing a nonprofit therapy dog program for underserved rural areas of North Carolina a reality. People who also possessed the power to crush her hopes, before the fledgling dream ever had a chance to get off the ground. This was her chance to prove herself.

Moose barked again.

She smiled at him. "It's your chance to show them what you can do, too."

At the sound of her voice, the dog's fluffy tail wriggled. Ready to go to work. As was she. Usually... She grimaced. Except Rob Melbourne was far from just any new client.

In the small town of Laurel Grove, everybody knew everybody. As children, their families had attended the same church. Handsome and effortlessly charming, Rob had been the golden boy of the football team. But he'd always been kind to everyone. Even a geeky brainiac like her.

After graduation, they'd gone their separate ways. According to her mom, who still lived in Laurel Grove, their adult lives had followed a similar trajectory. College. Marriage. And strangely enough, both of them widowed young. Rob's wife had died a few years ago.

Juliet wasn't sure why her mom believed it her duty to keep her updated on Laurel Grove happenings. Perhaps in the vain hope of one day convincing Juliet to return to her hometown for good.

She glanced around the neighborhood where Rob had grown up. For better or worse, she was back in Laurel Grove. At least for the foreseeable future.

Life had come full circle. Rob had proven himself not only a gridiron hero, but a real-life hero as well. The recent headline news about her old classmate hadn't surprised Juliet in the slightest. He was that kind of guy.

Even before saving those innocent people, his was the picture she would have put in the dictionary beside *hero*. Along with *swoonworthy*, *masculine* and a host of similarly themed adjectives.

Tall. Blond. Classically handsome with vivid blue eyes.

But suddenly feeling oddly disloyal to the memory of her late, beloved husband, she flushed.

The curtain on a window of the house next-door twitched. The neighbors were probably growing suspicious of her parked car. And after what the Melbournes had been through, she didn't blame them.

Juliet opened the door and got out. Coming around the car, she released Moose from the safety carrier in the back seat. She clicked the leash onto his collar.

She scooped up the dog and set him on the sidewalk. Moose stretched and then shook himself. When he tried pulling away on the leash, she frowned. It wasn't like him to be antsy.

Maybe her canine companion had picked up on her nervousness. The small dog had an uncanny sensitivity, an ability to read people's moods. It was what made him such a great therapy dog.

It had been a thirty-minute drive from Greensboro to the small-town community. Maybe Moose needed to work off any excess energy before their first meeting with the Melbournes. If only she could get over her own jitters so easily…

What was with her? She prided herself on her professionalism. Was it the man or the unusual aspects of this case that had her rattled?

She extended the leash to the edge of the lawn. Trotting over, Moose sniffed at the grass. She took a deep breath and made an attempt to relax.

Laurel Grove was at its best in May, and she enjoyed the feel of the sun on her bare arms. An unexpected bonus after the coldly clinical air of the children's wing.

Perhaps that's what it was—the change in setting had thrown her off her stride. Her previous cases had taken place in the hospital. But Rob had requested Paw Pals make an exception for him.

Juliet kept her gaze trained on Moose exploring every inch of the sidewalk. He must have detected the scent of another animal that had recently passed this way. A dog's ability to smell was between ten to one hundred thousand times greater than humans.

She didn't recall Rob being demanding, but life had a way of changing a person. As another condition of support therapy, he'd insisted on vetting the handler and dog before introducing them to his daughter. With his law enforcement background as a police detective, she hoped the interview didn't turn into an interrogation.

During high school, she'd had this silly schoolgirl crush on him. Not that he'd known she existed, of course. He'd been her first love. A totally unrequited first love.

But, despite her reservations regarding Rob Melbourne, the family liaison coordinator who'd supported her work to establish Paw Pals had urged her to take on the high-profile case.

Juliet's specialty was pediatrics. The one area where she and Rob's adult lives diverged. Thinking of the baby she'd miscarried, her heart pinched. An old sorrow.

However, she firmly believed good could come from even the worst of circumstances. While she had no children, she'd spent the last five years pouring herself and Moose into helping other people's children.

She tugged Moose closer. She needed to get more than just a grip on the leash. She wasn't seventeen anymore, and neither was Rob.

He was probably nothing like she remembered. She'd stopped watching the news when her late husband was deployed. And once she took on this case, she'd taken great pains to avoid watching the oft-broadcast video a bystander had recorded of Rob on the day of the shooting.

"So just stop it." She needed to get her resurgent adolescent insecurities in hand. "Stop it now."

Behind her on the sidewalk, a throat cleared. A deep, thoroughly masculine rasp. "Stop what?"

Swinging around, she gaped at him. Her heart did a strange sort of flutter against her rib cage.

Because the thirty-three-year-old version of Rob Melbourne was neither repulsive or ugly.

Just as she'd feared, far, far from it.

When the blue sedan pulled up to the curb, Rob took firm hold of the cane and painfully hauled himself to his feet from the porch step where he'd been waiting for the dog handler from Greensboro.

Thanks to the bullet wound he'd received after taking down the shooter, the days when he'd sprinted across a football field to Laurel Grove glory were but a distant memory. Blessed since childhood with an innate blend of athleticism and strength, he'd taken mobility for granted. But now each step required an enormous amount of forethought.

And a strength of an entirely different sort.

Gingerly, he negotiated the descent to the ground. He'd discovered balance was a tricky thing. And gravity wasn't always his friend.

When the woman behind the wheel didn't immediately get out of the car, he'd moved toward the driveway to intercept her. With his four-year-old daughter asleep in the house, he preferred to conduct this initial assessment of the therapy dog outdoors. He was anxious to put this lingering ordeal behind them as soon as possible.

Neither he nor Sophie were sleeping well at night.

This afternoon, he'd held her in his arms until she finally drifted into sleep. But her peaceful slumber wouldn't last long.

Since the active shooter incident at the shopping center last month in Greensboro, it never did. Soon she'd awaken, shrieking in terror.

Though physically unharmed by what happened that day, she hadn't come through unscathed. She remained a fragile, too-quiet shell of the bubbly, happy little girl she'd been. Unable to break through to Sophie, the hospital's child psychologist had recommended the services of a new pilot program, Paw Pals.

He was at his wit's end. If this canine emotional support program didn't work… His gut clenched.

The one time he'd lowered his guard and relaxed his usual occupational vigilance had proven disastrous. He wouldn't make that mistake again. If the handler and dog weren't the right fit for Sophie, more harm than good would result.

He couldn't afford to get his hopes up. Too much was at stake. The family liaison coordinator set up the appointment with a Juliet Newkirk, founder of the Paw Pals program. The name caught his attention.

The only Juliet he'd ever known was Juliet Mitchell from high school. Not Newkirk. Probably not the same person.

Leaning heavily on the cane, he shifted the bulk of his weight onto his good leg. Moving like an old man, he shuffled toward the sidewalk at the bottom of the drive.

A soft breeze wafted through the pines. Overhead, the sky arched a brilliant blue. The scent of his late mother's lilac shrub floated across his nostrils. Laurel Grove was ablaze with the colors of spring.

The woman had gotten out of her car with the canine. At his approach, the pint-size dog stilled. But the woman had her back to him, talking and gesturing with her hands.

He couldn't see her face, but he took the opportunity to get a quick, unobserved read on the person who was supposed to bring healing to his traumatized child.

Based on his six-foot stature, he estimated her to be about five foot six. Long, dark hair cascaded past her shoulders. In accordance with the balmy day, she wore a short-sleeve, light purple shirt and jean capris. A fanny pack was clipped around her slender waist. Maybe full of dog treats.

Who *was* she talking to? Except for the loose leash, her hands were free. Perhaps she was speaking to someone on her cell phone? Or to the dog?

Attention riveted on Rob, the white dog with the black head, tan splotches and large dark eyes cocked his head, staring at him, the strange man with the stick.

Rob caught the tail end of her words. "Stop what?"

Jerking, she spun around.

His heart inexplicably ticked up a notch. "Juliet Mitchell. I wondered if it might be you. I always thought your name unusual. And pretty."

He clamped his jaw shut, not sure why he'd added the last part. But at his words, something flickered across her expressive, dark brown eyes. Gone too quickly for him to interpret.

Somewhere from underneath a bush, a robin trilled.

"You probably don't remember me." He was aware he was starting to ramble, which wasn't like him. "We went to high school together."

Another inscrutable look flashed across her features. "I remember."

Her voice was soft, melodic. The dog sat on his haunches

at her feet. He wore a purple canine vest, embroidered with the gold Paw Pals logo and the words Therapy Dog.

"Nice to see you again. I'm Juliet Newkirk now." She extended her hand.

When his fingers touched hers, a spark flew up his arm. Her eyes widened. *She'd felt that, too, huh?* He let go of her hand.

Yet his eyes flitted to her bare ring finger. Usually women wore their wedding rings, but maybe she was divorced. And he wasn't sure what irritated him more.

That he'd looked, or his attraction to her. Weird, unsettling. Probably time for another pain pill for his leg. Although what that had to do with the tingle in his arm, he preferred not to examine too closely.

"Let's talk on the porch." He gestured toward the house. "Sophie's asleep right now. I need to stick close in case she needs me."

Juliet followed him. "Come." At her command, the dog pitter-pattered after them, tail wagging. Scampering to keep pace with their longer strides.

Rob stopped at the bottom of the steps. His leg throbbed. No need to attempt to climb his personal Mount Everest until he had to.

She lifted her palm to the dog. "Sit."

Once again, the dog parked himself alongside his owner. Rob was impressed with her control of the canine. But the dog left him decidedly underwhelmed.

Leaning against the handrail for support, he jabbed his finger at the tiny animal. "That's the therapy dog that's supposed to help my daughter?"

"This is Moose. Say hello, Moose."

Lifting his head, the dog yipped twice.

"Moose?" Rob narrowed his eyes. "That dog can't weigh more than five pounds. Or do you mean *m-o-u-s-e*?"

Her smile flattened. "I assure you *M-o-o-s-e* is a highly trained certified therapy dog, Mr. Melbourne."

"Please call me Rob." He scratched his neck. "Moose is one of those froufrou purse dogs, isn't he?"

She stiffened. "What were you expecting?"

He shrugged. "I've worked in police departments with K-9 units. Those dogs were larger, more intelligent breeds like German shepherds, Malinois and Rottweilers."

She gave him an irritated look. "Intelligence and size are not mutually exclusive. Because of his size, most children find Moose less intimidating."

"What breed is he exactly?"

She flipped her hair over her shoulder. "I can't be sure, but the vet and I believe—"

"What do you mean you can't be sure?"

She lifted her chin. "Moose is a rescue dog. He's a mixture of Chihuahua, terrier and most likely some—"

"You got that dog from a shelter?" His jaw worked. "What about his background?"

"We suspect Moose was bred in a puppy mill and experienced his own trauma before being abandoned and eventually placed in the shelter."

Rob drew himself up. "You expect me to expose my daughter to a dog you don't know anything about?"

She took a step toward him. "Because of his background, Moose has a rare sensitivity to hurting people. He's extremely obedient and well-behaved."

"I can see that," Rob admitted with reluctance. "But what's with those crazy batwing ears of his?"

She pursed her lips. "That's the papillon part I was trying to tell you about."

Letting the cane rest against the railing, he folded his arms. "I won't apologize for being protective of Sophie."

"Nor should you. But Moose and I are both used to

being underestimated. What Moose lacks in stature he more than makes up for in empathy. I think the only true size worth measuring is the size of his compassion. Small dog, big heart."

Small woman, big determination.

Juliet opened her hands. "Please give him—give us—a chance to help your daughter. He's worked nearly seventy-five successful cases with children."

"I don't think this is going to work." He raked his hand over his head. "I'm sorry to have dragged you over here for nothing. But—"

"Daddy?" From inside the house, a child's voice wailed.

His gaze snapped to the door. "I'm on the porch, Soph." His stomach knotted. "Daddy's coming."

Juliet turned toward the house. At her feet, Moose's ears perked forward.

"Where are you, Daddy?" the child cried. "I can't find you. Don't leave me."

Rob flinched as if she'd struck him. "Don't be afraid, honey." He grabbed his cane. "Hang on. I'm coming."

He lifted his foot to the step. "I'm all she's got." Swinging his wounded leg around, he inhaled sharply.

Leaping forward, Juliet reached for his arm. "Let me help."

He shook her off. "I don't need your—"

"What's a dog doing at our house, Daddy?"

Tail swishing, Moose barked at the door. She and Rob looked at the little girl, standing on the other side of the screen.

And something entirely unexpected turned over in Juliet's heart.

Sophie was small with delicate, fragile features. Her

long, dark brown hair framed a sweet, heart-shaped face. Juliet guessed she must resemble her mother. But she shared one particular trait with her dad. They both possessed the same startling blue eyes.

The child inched closer to the screen. "Ooohhh. He's so cute, Daddy." She clapped her hands. "His ears look like butterfly wings."

"Butterflies, not bats." Juliet cut her eyes at Rob. "A case of beauty being in the eye of the beholder."

He had the grace to chuckle. "Clearly." He pulled himself onto the porch.

Sophie pushed her face against the screen. "What's the doggie's name?"

Juliet and Moose remained on the bottom step, waiting for her father's permission to approach.

"Haven't seen her this animated in a month of Sundays." He motioned. "Be my guest. Here's your chance."

She smiled. "Come."

Moose skittered up the steps.

"Hi, Sophie." She stopped beside Rob. "My name is Juliet. And this is Moose."

Recognizing his name, the little dog barked twice and pranced closer to the screen.

Sophie dropped to a crouch. "That's a silly name for a little dog." She smiled up at Juliet. "But it fits him."

"I think you're right."

Waggling his backside, Moose did a complete turn as if chasing his feather duster tail.

Juliet rolled her eyes. "Now you're just showing off, circus clown." But she grinned at the tiny dog.

Sophie laid her palm flat against the screen. "He's a happy dog."

Moose's tongue darted out, trying to lick her through the mesh. She giggled.

"Yes, he is." Juliet's gaze flicked to Sophie's father. Once again, seeking his unspoken permission.

He gave her a curt nod.

She turned toward his daughter. "Would you like to come outside and pet him, Sophie?"

Eyes rounding, the child shrank back. "I can't go outside." She shook her head. Strands of hair whiplashed her pale cheeks. "It isn't safe," she whispered.

"She won't leave the house." Rob scrubbed his hand over his face. "I don't know how to help her. Or how to make it better."

The look of anguish on his rugged features gutted Juliet. This family had been through so much. Sensing the child's turmoil, Moose whined softly and strained forward against the screen.

"Would you allow Moose and I to try?" Juliet touched Rob's arm. "Would you let us help you to help her?"

"Sophie seems taken with your dog. And with you. She needs help." Under the cotton shirt, his broad shoulders slumped. "I need your help."

A natural leader, driven to succeed, he wasn't a man who easily revealed vulnerability. For him to admit he needed help was no small thing.

"Moose loves children. Children love him. We'll do everything we can to help Sophie recover."

Gratitude flooded his remarkable eyes. "Thank you."

"I read the case file, but I didn't understand the extent of Sophie's fear until now." Juliet straightened. "It may require multiple playdates with Moose before we make any breakthroughs. Be prepared for the long haul."

"We'll be available anytime, any day that works with your schedule." He reached to open the door. "At least, living in Laurel Grove you won't have to travel far." He held the door for her.

Thinking of her apartment in Greensboro, she paused on the threshold.

Sophie scrambled to her feet. "Can I pet him? Can I show Moose my room? Can I—"

"Slow down, Sophie girl."

Her father laughed, the rumbling sound rusty like he was out of practice. But it resonated deep within Juliet. Electrifying her nerve endings.

When her husband, Josh, died it was like something vital inside her fell asleep. For the first time in five years, she felt herself awakening. And just as when a limb falls asleep, the pins and needles of coming to life proved to be both exhilarating and painful.

It was time. Long past time. How ironic her first teenage love should bring her to this realization.

But she wasn't ready. She was happy with her life—with Moose and their work. She didn't want or need to move on. Because when she did, she'd lose Josh forever.

Her pulse raced. Coming here had been a mistake. She should leave.

Sophie hopped from one foot to another. "Can I touch him, Daddy? Can I hold him, Miss Juliet?"

Juliet glanced from the child's hopeful face to her father's. "Climb on the couch," she finally said. "He'll come to you."

Across the room, Sophie scrambled onto the well-worn, comfortable sofa. Juliet released Moose. The little dog raced over to the child. His small legs ate up the distance. His paws scrabbled at the base of the sofa.

"You'll have to lift him onto the couch, Sophie." Juliet coiled the leash around her forearm. "He can't get there without your help."

Sophie picked Moose off the floor and settled him in

her lap. Juliet remained frozen where she stood, unable to move forward or backward.

A metaphor for her life?

Rob let the door fall shut behind them. "What's wrong?"

"Nothing." She sighed. "Sophie, stroke Moose gently. He likes to be petted on his head, his back and behind his ears."

Giving Juliet a tentative smile, Sophie did as she was instructed. Curled over his body, Moose's tail swished happily.

Rob took a breath. "Thank you."

She looked at him. "For what?"

"For giving Sophie back her smile." His voice was thick with emotion.

A lump rose in her throat. Rob joined his daughter on the couch with Moose. Her heart did a treacherous lurch. What was it about the man that affected her so?

She was afraid the more time she spent with her hero, the more she would... What? Enjoy his company? Have to acknowledge her loneliness?

After Josh died, she'd sworn off romantic relationships for good. And her strategy had been working great. Until she met Rob Melbourne again.

She sank into the armchair, close enough to converse with the family, or to intervene if circumstances necessitated it. She fisted the leash.

Getting to know the real Rob might prove more hazardous to her carefully constructed barricades than the teenage Rob of her adolescent imaginings.

A tremulous joy slowly stole over the little girl's face. This wasn't about Juliet and maintaining her comfort zone. This was about bringing wholeness to a hurting child. She couldn't ignore the need of Rob's daughter. Not when it was within her ability to help.

For Sophie's sake, Juliet could move in with her mom for a couple of weeks. She and Moose would visit the Melbournes every day. The sooner Sophie returned to normal, the better.

And in the meantime, she'd have to be very careful to guard her heart around Sophie's dad.

Rob laughed at something Sophie said to Moose. Juliet swallowed, hard.

Easier said than done.

Chapter Two

As she pulled open the glass-fronted door, the bell jangled. Juliet stepped into her mom's knitting shop on Main Street.

Seated on the comfy gray couch and in the cluster of armchairs, three older women turned their attention from their knitting needles toward the door.

Juliet bit back a sigh. She'd forgotten today was the weekly gathering of the Knit-Knack Club.

The three women were charter club members and her mother's best friends. It wasn't that Juliet didn't love these ladies—she did—but encountered as a pack they could be overwhelming.

Nestled in the crook of her arm, Moose let out a welcoming bark. The women's faces transformed into broad smiles.

She'd known these women her entire life. Both a good thing and a bad thing. The knitters didn't only help each other untangle snarls in the yarn. They also doled out "purls" of wisdom for unsnarling the tangles of life.

Whether you asked for their advice or not.

Sixty and never-met-a-stranger, Evelyn Gilmer fluttered her fingers at Moose. "There's my favorite doggy-woggy."

Juliet hid a smile. The little therapy dog brought out the baby talk in people.

Retired school administrator Geraldine Stancil laid aside her knitting. "Let me see that sweet little thing."

The oldest of the group at seventy-five, the always immaculately turned out Helen Davidson patted Geraldine's thigh. "Age before beauty, Geri."

Her dark cheeks lifting, Geraldine laughed. "Flattery will get you nowhere, old friend."

Wearing jeans and a pale blue sweater over a long-sleeve white shirt, Juliet's mom glanced up from the register and smiled. "Hello, darling."

At least one person was glad to see her and not just Moose. Although she really didn't mind—she was the original member of the Moose fan club. Knowing better than to play favorites, she set the small dog on the coffee table in front of the ladies.

Her mother believed that any knit shop worth its needles offered a place to sit, knit and announce new grandbabies, too. Customers didn't only craft scarves or sweaters. At Ewe Made Me Luv You, they crafted community.

A retired pastor's wife, Helen leaned forward and quickly scooped him into her lap. "All's fair in love and Moose, Geri."

The two old friends grinned at each other. This was where the knitters of Laurel Grove gathered to share their joys and sorrows. And to create something beautiful together.

Juliet rested on the arm of the sofa while her mom finished waiting on the customer. "What project are you ladies working on today, Miss Evelyn?"

In the South, it was considered good manners to address any woman who was your elder as Miss. The sudden memory of Sophie calling her Miss Juliet caused her to smile.

Evelyn held up her project. "Pillows to cushion the ports where cancer patients receive their chemo treatment."

Last time Juliet was home, they'd been knitting modesty shawls for nursing mothers.

"Haven't seen you in a while." Geraldine peered at Juliet over the rim of her hot-pink readers. "I guess city life keeps you pretty busy."

Called on the carpet by her former high school principal, Juliet did her best not to squirm. Or feel seventeen again.

She flushed. "Yes, ma'am. Work and Moose."

"Juliet's work is important. She helps people." Evelyn patted her hand. "It's good to see you, sweetie." Her big, blue eyes reminded Juliet of Rob.

Not surprising since Evelyn was his aunt. Small-town life was just that—small. And intricately interconnected.

Juliet gave her a one-armed hug. When she "grew up," she wanted silver hair just like the still-very-youthful Evelyn.

The other two women continued to coo over the tiny mutt.

Evelyn held on to her for a half second longer than Juliet expected. "However, don't forget you only get one mama," she whispered.

Juliet stiffened. "What's wrong with Mom?"

But just then the customer exited. Swooping in, the stack of silver bracelets on her wrists jingling, her mother draped her arm around Juliet's shoulders. "Excuse us, ladies, I'm going to borrow my best girl for a moment to help me restock a few shelves."

Still ignoring everyone but Moose, Geraldine made a vague, away-with-you motion. Miss Helen didn't bother looking up from the toy dog.

As her mom whisked her away, Juliet cast a quick glance over her shoulder at Evelyn. Pressing her lips together, the older woman gave Juliet a slight shake of her head.

The walls of the shop were lined with a rainbow assortment of hand-dyed, specialty yarns on shelves. Display tables with knitting-themed gifts, kits and patterns dotted the store. Essential tools for every conceivable type of fiber art hung from a nearby stand.

Her mother handed Juliet a lavender skein from the cardboard box at their feet. "How did it go this morning with Rob and Sophie?" She pushed the sleeves of her shirt to her elbows.

"I never said I was meeting with the Melbournes."

She'd called her mom last night to let her know she was coming to Laurel Grove for a client meeting and would drop by the Ewe later.

"You didn't have to tell me." Her mother placed a skein as blue-green as the ocean into one of the cubbyholes along the yarn wall. "Rob told Evelyn about his appointment with Paw Pals. Evelyn told me this morning."

She made a face. "So much for client confidentiality."

Her mom chuckled. "This is Laurel Grove, darling."

With more force than strictly necessary, she shoved a cloud-soft bundle of lemony yellow into the appropriate slot. "Where nobody knows how to mind their own business."

After Josh's death, that was her primary reason for not returning to her hometown.

Her mother's brow puckered. "They don't mean any harm. They simply care so much."

She gritted her teeth. "There is such a thing as caring too much."

"Before you get your doggie biscuits in a twist…" Her mom arched her brow. "You have Evelyn to thank for convincing Rob to give Paw Pals a try in the first place."

Wrinkling her brow, she helped her mother empty the carton.

Hands on her hips, her mom stood back to survey their handiwork. "Everyone was so thankful Rob and Sophie survived the shooting. But they still have a long road to complete recovery."

Juliet could see herself reflected in the lenses of her mother's large, brown glasses. She'd been told her entire life she resembled her mom. Behind the frames, her mom's dark brown eyes—so like Juliet's own—mirrored concern.

"What do you mean?"

"Rob's recovery has been sporadic because Sophie hasn't been able to let him out of her sight." With the tip of her finger, Juliet's mother pushed her glasses higher on the bridge of her nose. "Physical therapy is at a standstill. Evelyn is the only one besides Rob that Sophie feels comfortable with these days."

Rob was very close to his aunt. Evelyn and her husband had finished raising him after his parents died.

Her mom tucked a tendril of dark brown hair with its glints of silver behind her ear. "You've decided to take the case?"

As long as Juliet could remember, her mother had worn her hair in an easy, modern pixie cut, which emphasized the high cheekbones Juliet had inherited.

"Sophie seemed very taken with Moose. But it's going

to require more intense and prolonged interaction than with my usual clients. Because of their unique situation, possibly back-to-back sessions in their home." She bit her lip. "I was wondering if I could camp out at your house for a few weeks to be more accessible to Sophie."

Her mom's eyes brightened. "What a wonderful idea. It'll give us a chance to catch up."

Guilt stabbed Juliet. Was this what Miss Evelyn had meant? Was her mother lonely?

When was the last time she'd seen her mom? A few weeks ago, on Mother's Day, she'd taken her mom out for lunch to a fancy place in Greensboro. And before that? Easter.

They talked every couple of days on the phone or texted, but the sheer delight on her mother's face at the prospect of spending time together made her feel ashamed. Entangled in her grief and caught up in getting Paw Pals established, too often she'd taken her mom for granted. Miss Geraldine was right to call her to task for her neglect.

"We can do movie marathons at night. Eat popcorn by the handfuls. And gallons of ice cream by the tub. I'll fix your favorite meals." Her mother clasped her hands together under her chin. "Just us girls. Just like old times."

Juliet blinked back sudden moisture in her eyes. "That sounds great, Mom. I can't wait." She threw her arms around her mother. A faint scent of roses clung to her mom.

Suddenly, she became painfully aware of how slight her mother felt in her arms. Lesley Mitchell had always been elegantly thin, tall and willowy. But there was a fragility there now that hadn't been there before.

Releasing her, Juliet scanned her mom's features. Were

there purple shadows under her eyes? "Have you been sleeping okay? Is something wrong?"

"What could be wrong?" Her mother brushed a quick hand underneath her eyes. "My beautiful daughter is coming home for a visit. I'm ecstatic."

Her mom hadn't truly answered her question, yet willing to be convinced, she squeezed her mother's arm.

Nothing but skin and bones. She frowned. Living alone, she knew how easy it was to not eat properly. While she was in Laurel Grove, she'd make sure her mom ate more nutritious meals.

Cushioned between bouts of movie popcorn and ice cream naturally.

"It'll be fun." Juliet took a cleansing breath. "First, though, I need to run to my condo to pack a suitcase. I'll be back for supper. How about I fix dinner tonight?"

"Text me the ingredients, and I'll head to the grocery after closing." Her mother grinned. "It's a go," she called to someone over Juliet's shoulder.

Juliet whipped around. Evelyn put a hand to her heart. The other two ladies replied with their own thumbs-up gesture. Moose let out an excited bark.

"Mom!" Juliet grabbed her mother's hand. "The Melbournes don't need anyone broadcasting their difficulties to the world."

"Not the world." Her mom tilted her head. "Just the folks who've cared for them since a suddenly single dad brought his baby daughter to Laurel Grove two years ago and found a home for them both."

Juliet swallowed. Her home had been with Josh. Where they'd laughed and loved and planned a future that never happened. She'd known no home since men in uniform rang her doorbell that awful day five years ago. Home and Josh were lost to her forever.

Her mom unpacked another colorful skein. "Besides, the instant your car pulled up to the curb, half the neighborhood called to let us know you'd arrived."

"I don't think it's too much to ask everyone to respect their privacy and mine."

Her mother motioned toward the Knit-Knack Club. "We've been praying you and Moose would be able to help them."

Some of the starch went out of Juliet. Their interference was motivated by love. "Sophie's well-being could rest on the outcome of this case."

Her mom's eyes glinted. "Sophie isn't the only one hurting."

Juliet raised her eyebrow. "You mean Rob?"

Her mother folded her arms across her sweater. Too warm to wear on a May day in North Carolina. "Not just Rob."

"You mean me? Me and Rob?" She gasped. "Tell me you and the Knit-Knack Club haven't cooked up some ridiculous scheme to—"

"Would it be so ridiculous?"

Laughably so. Even without the separate baggage of bereavement each of them carried, the likelihood of her and Rob Melbourne ever ending up together was as likely as... As...

"It's been five years since Josh died."

"Exactly. It's only been five years." Juliet threw out her hands. "I don't need you and the town pressuring me to date again. This is why I had to—"

Her mother's face fell, knowing why she'd not returned to Laurel Grove.

The town's well-intentioned sympathy hadn't helped her deal with her grief. Their efforts to make her feel better had only made her feel worse.

"What is it you need from us, Juliet?" Her mom's voice went soft and low.

"Same as before. Space." She sighed. "And time."

"Is time and space working for you?"

Juliet raised her chin. "I'm better. Really I am." She'd only cried herself to sleep once last week.

Her mother looked at her a long, slow moment. "Whatever you say, darling." She touched a hand to Juliet's cheek. "Space and time. We'll follow your lead. You're the professional." She ambled toward the back of the store.

Juliet stared after her. If only that were true. But not in Laurel Grove. Here she'd always be Lesley Mitchell's fatherless little girl. The geeky, awkward teenager. The brave Marine's tragic, young widow.

She moved to collect Moose from his adoring fans. At the sight of her, his tail swished with glee.

A smile tugged at her lips. She was Moose's human mom, too. Which these days was, by far, her favorite title.

Calling out her goodbyes, she took her leave of the Knit-Knack Club and headed out of the shop. After securing Moose in the car, she steered down Main Street toward the highway out of town. Laurel Grove and nearby Greensboro were located in the rolling hill country of North Carolina's Piedmont Triad region, which also included High Point and Winston-Salem.

It wasn't a hard drive. Easily doable every day for her sessions with Sophie, but something whispered to her she needed to be closer. To be available at a moment's notice. That's when most breakthroughs happened.

When you least expected them.

Concern for her mother niggled at the edges of her mind. Until she got to the bottom of what was going on with her mom, proximity to Laurel Grove might prove of even greater importance.

In the distance, she spotted the familiar outline of downtown Greensboro's tallest buildings. The city was conveniently situated between the misty blue horizon of the Blue Ridge Mountains to the west and the sandy Atlantic beaches of the Outer Banks to the east.

She veered onto an exit ramp onto Battleground Avenue and turned into her neighborhood off Lawndale. She parked outside her apartment building. Slinging her purse over her arm, she released Moose and carried the small canine up the three flights of stairs.

Inserting the key, she quickly stepped inside, which set off the high-pitched security alarm. Hating the noise, Moose tensed but per his training made no other reaction.

Setting him onto his feet, she shut off the shrieking noise. Moose pattered over to his brown doggie cushion in the kitchen. She'd only been gone since this morning, but the darkened, shuttered one-bedroom condo had a hollow feel to it.

As if no one had lived here for a very long time.

She switched on the overhead lights. The condo wasn't home. It was simply a place to sleep.

Juliet cut her eyes to her wedding photo on the mantel in the living room. Such a happy, happy day. After losing Josh, the apartment had become her sanctuary from the world.

If she were honest, more than a sanctuary. A place to mark time until one day she could be with Josh again. But she was young. She was healthy. In all probability, that day would be decades from now.

She missed him so much. She'd been floundering in sadness with no real purpose until Moose came into her life. Without the little dog and their work, she didn't know how she'd bear the empty years that loomed ahead.

Even so, some days were better than others.

In the bedroom, she pulled out a suitcase from the walk-in closet. She transferred essential items from the bathroom and clothing from the bureau. She'd need to pack Moose's things, too.

Almost as if summoned by her thoughts, there was the pitter-patter of toenails across the linoleum as Moose followed her into the bedroom. Such a good, good dog. He somehow always knew when she was hurting the most.

Juliet scooped him into her arms. Holding the small canine close to her heart, she buried her nose in his fur. She and Moose did important work. Work that made a difference in the lives of many hurting children.

She took a deep, cleansing breath. Time to once again set aside her own grief and concentrate on helping others find the wholeness that had proven so elusive to her in the days since Josh's death.

Nuzzling her face in Moose's fur, she hoped Moose could bring Sophie the same comfort he'd given her. And as for her illogical feelings of attraction for Sophie's father?

Juliet had nearly given up hope of ever knowing peace again.

Love proving almost as impossible to find as home.

Chapter Three

The next morning, hearing a car in the driveway, Rob hurried to the window. Drawing aside the curtain, he spotted Juliet getting out of her vehicle.

He glanced over his shoulder at his daughter sitting at the kitchen table. It had been a virtually sleepless night. Neither one of them were moving much beyond a snail's pace.

Sophie hunkered over a plate of pancakes he had cooked to entice her flagging appetite. Discouragement hung over both of them like a haze.

God, please help Juliet and her therapy dog to make a difference.

At the click of toenails outside on the porch steps, Sophie's head jerked. "Is that Moose and Miss Juliet?" Jumping up, she dashed over and yanked the door open before Rob could intercept her.

Leash in hand, Juliet had her fist raised to knock. She was casually dressed in khaki capris and slip-on sandals. The pink shirt brought out the color of her cheeks.

Sophie threw her arms around the dog handler's waist. "I missed you." In her exuberance, she almost knocked Juliet off her feet.

He reached for his daughter. "Careful, Soph. Let Miss Juliet come inside before you tackle her."

But Juliet's arms came around the child. "I missed you, too. Moose is very excited to play with you today."

Tail swishing, Moose barked. He scampered into the house.

Sophie's face underwent a transformation. "Hey, Moose. Remember me?" She squatted beside the little mutt.

Moose licked her chin, and she giggled.

"I'm so excited to play with you, Moose." Sophie's gaze flicked to Juliet. "It's boring to stay inside with Daddy. But it's safer."

His heart wrenched.

Juliet touched the top of Sophie's head. "No boredom allowed today. Moose wants to show you a few tricks he's been practicing."

Rob bit back a laugh at the expression on Sophie's face.

"Ooohhh… Moose does tricks." Her smile widened. "Isn't that cool, Daddy?" Standing, she gripped his hand.

For a moment, she was once again the sweet, never-met-a-stranger child he'd loved since the day she was born. In that split second, Sophie seemed to be the very image of her late mother. The little girl was Katrina's best and final gift to him.

His eyes misted. "The coolest."

Sophie latched on to Juliet. "Can Daddy watch Moose do his tricks, too?"

Juliet smiled. "The more the merrier."

"Yay!" Letting go of them, Sophie skipped over to the sofa.

Juliet deposited a large purple backpack beside the armchair.

"I've never seen Sophie take as quickly to anyone as she has to you."

Juliet unclipped her furry companion from the leash. The small canine set off like a shot toward Sophie. "Who can help loving Moose?"

Rob closed the front door and joined them. "Not just Moose."

Taking a brush out of the backpack, she handed it to Sophie. "Would you do me the biggest favor and brush Moose's fur? He likes to look his best before doing his tricks. It soothes him. I know you'll be gentle. Start at his head and work down."

Delighted, Sophie scooped Moose up to the sofa. She brushed the tiny dog with broad, even strokes. "Like this, Miss Juliet?" Moose snuggled against her, crawling into her lap.

Juliet laid her palm on Sophie's hair. "Exactly like that. Aren't you the gentlest, kindest girl to take such good care of him?"

"Miss Juliet says I'm a great hair brusher, Daddy."

Grinning, he leaned against the sofa. "I think Sophie's just proved my point. You've made a strong impression all your own, Juliet."

She laughed. "Not sure that's a good thing or not."

"Definitely a good thing." He fingered his chin. "You've always made a good impression on everyone."

A crease furrowed the space between her eyebrows. "Really? I'm surprised you think so."

"Why would you say that?"

She shrugged. "Back in high school, I didn't realize you even knew my name."

"Laurel Grove High isn't that big. Then or now." He frowned. "Of course, I knew who you were."

"We didn't exactly run in the same circles."

He eased into his leather recliner and put up the foot-rest. He'd been up for hours and on his injured leg too long. "You make me sound like a conceited jock."

It stung him more than it should that she had such a low opinion of him. And disturbed him even more that it should matter so much.

She scrutinized his propped leg. "Are you in pain?"

"I'm okay," he grunted.

His gaze darted to Sophie, but she was completely engaged in fluffing Moose's fur just so.

The canine wasn't the only one soothed by the rhyth-mic strokes of the hairbrush. Sophie's tight, hunched shoulders, another by-product of the shooting, had re-laxed. Her face had lost the pinched, anxious look.

Juliet's forehead creased. "Why don't I believe you?"

"Until we're able to resolve our current—" he pursed his lips "—situation, I'm unable to visit the physical ther-apist at the hospital. He made a home visit last week and left me some exercises to strengthen my leg muscles."

"Just don't overdo it." She perched on the edge of the chair, her hands on her knees. "And for the record, I never considered you a conceited jock. You were nice to everyone, including someone like me."

"I don't know what you mean by 'someone like you.'"

"Like I said, we didn't run in the same circles. I wasn't a cheerleader or athletic."

"You were senior class president. Voted Most Likely to Achieve. And best I recall, you were almost single-handedly responsible for what is still reputed to be the best junior-senior prom to ever grace Laurel Grove High."

She fluttered her hand. "An entire committee put the prom together. Not just me."

"You chaired the honor club." He counted off on his fingers. "You were a peer buddy to students with disabilities. A Habitat for Humanity volunteer. Headed the Future Business Leaders club. And in my opinion perhaps your most remarkable achievement was when you led the 4-H to a regional victory." He grinned at her. "You lived in town, not on a farm, and yet somehow managed to raise a prizewinning, blue-ribbon calf."

"JoJo." She blushed. "I've always loved animals. I can't believe you remembered that about me."

"Aunt Evie and your mom are best friends. JoJo the calf lived on Uncle Adrian's farm. You visited every day after school to take care of him."

"You weren't exactly idle, either. Mr. Running Back, who took us to a state championship."

"Of course, I noticed you. You were so involved and busy. Class valedictorian."

"Classic overachiever. Type A on steroids." She raised her hand palm up. "The nerdy brainiac. That's me." A tinge of red crept up her neck beneath the pink collar of her cotton shirt.

Is that how she saw herself? He hadn't meant to embarrass her. The opposite, in fact.

Unlike some of the shallow female acquaintances in his circle, he'd always been slightly intrigued by the quiet force of nature known as Juliet Mitchell. Still waters run deep, Uncle Adrian used to say.

More than a little intimidating to the teenage boy he'd once been. Only now did he realize Juliet was shy. Probably still was.

"You're the smartest girl I ever knew. I admired your energy and drive." He scratched his head. "A trait we shared."

She gave him a smile. "An enormous compliment from a guy who's made it his life mission to make the world a safer place. Thank you for your service." She motioned toward his leg. "Even if it almost cost you your life."

"Maybe it's time to rethink my life mission. Considering where that's landed us." His eyes flitted to his oblivious daughter, entranced by her new doggie friend. His shoulders slumped.

"That's why we're here." Juliet sat forward. "To help you get through this. On the other side of the trauma, there is a better place."

He swallowed. "You know this for sure? From personal experience? Aunt Evie told me about your husband."

Something sharp, raw, filled her eyes, cutting him to the quick.

"I… I can't talk about Josh." She looked away, unable to meet his gaze. "I'm not at that better place yet. But I have to keep believing it exists, and that one day I'll get there myself." Her eyes darted to Sophie. "I was drowning at first. It was Moose who saved me. He kept me putting one foot in front of the other. Giving me a reason to get out of bed to take care of him."

"Same for me with Soph."

Juliet turned to him.

He gave her a sad smile. "See, I told you we have more in common than you think."

She stared at him. The moment pulsed between them. Fraught with a visceral electricity. And something he wasn't ready to put a name to.

Abruptly, she stood. An expression of near panic flickered across her delicate features.

"Moose." She clapped her hand against her thigh. "Let's show Sophie and Mr. Melbourne what you can do."

Ears perking, the therapy dog jumped off the sofa.

Back to Mr. Melbourne again? Rob felt the barrier

she erected between them like a physical blow. Or a door closing.

The door to her heart.

It wasn't like her to expose her feelings—most definitely not her pain—to someone who was practically a stranger.

But Rob had a way of flying under the radar of her defense mechanisms. Impossible to ignore. Getting under her skin.

In front of the sofa, she crouched beside her furry comrade. Body shimmying, Moose nuzzled against her.

Rob was merely a guy she knew a long time ago. Someone who needed Moose's help. Once this assignment was over, she'd return to her real life in Greensboro. Rob and his adorable daughter would resume theirs.

As for that second when he'd looked at her...

The moment had strayed into a realm she'd not anticipated. Almost as if they'd seen each other's loss and recognized something familiar in each other. A connection.

Which was totally unacceptable. Absolutely unprofessional. And terrifying.

After Josh's death, she'd never allowed herself to be attracted to any man. Until now?

"What kind of tricks does Moose do, Miss Juliet?"

Brought out of her painful musings, she smiled at Sophie. "I'm going to let Moose show you. Lie down, Moose."

Her canine companion went onto his belly.

"Show Sophie how old you are, Moose."

Moose lifted his left front paw and brought it down on the area rug.

"One..."

Moose tapped the rug again.

"Two." Juliet continued to count as his paw stroked the floor. "Three. Good boy."

She handed the dog a small treat from the bag she kept clipped around her waist when working. Moose gobbled it up quickly. "Moose is three years old."

Giggling, Sophie came off the couch and dropped onto her stomach beside the dog. "Do you know how old I am, Moose?" She slapped the rug with the palm of her hand. "One. Two."

Rob chuckled. "What are you doing, Sophie?"

Juliet's lips twitched.

"Three. Four. I'm four years old." Sophie held up four fingers. "I'm doing Moose-talk, Daddy."

Despite her resolve to hold herself aloof from Sophie's dad, Juliet's eyes flicked to him.

Catching her gaze, he gave her a lopsided smile. "Do all your kid clients speak Moose?"

She smiled. "This is a first."

Grinning, he rubbed the back of his neck. "Leave it to Sophie."

But Juliet felt immeasurably cheered by Sophie's identification with Moose. And consequently for Sophie's chances of working through the trauma.

Juliet got off her knees. "Roll over and dance, Moose."

Obediently, the dog did a rollover and then, springing up, he did a funny, front-paws-up dance while balancing on his hind legs.

Sophie clapped.

Rob ran his hand over his head. "That's one impressive dog."

She loved it when people appreciated her canine co-worker. "Good boy, Moose. Good boy."

Moose dropped to all fours. Holding another treat pinched between her thumb and finger, she rewarded him. She threw Rob a glance. "Ever seen a dog do the moonwalk?"

His eyebrows arched. "You're kidding me, right?"

She fluttered her lashes at him. "Watch and be amazed."

At her signal, Moose crept backward, his paws sliding across the carpet.

Sophie leaped up. "Can I try? Let me try."

Much to Juliet's amusement, the little girl and the little dog made a giant, backward circle around the sofa.

"Come on, Daddy." Sophie beckoned. "You do it, too. With me and Moosie."

Rob's eyes widened. "Me?"

"Yeah, Mr. All-State Running Back." Juliet smirked. "Let's see you moonwalk with Sophie and Moose." Her gaze fell to his leg. "Oh. I'm sorry. You shouldn't—"

With a snap, he brought the recliner forward, closing the footrest. "You don't think I can do it, do you?" His to-die-for blue eyes sparked.

Her nerve endings pinged like raindrops on a hot tin roof. Feeling weak in the knees, she sank onto the sofa.

She'd forgotten about his competitive streak. Had there ever been a challenge he'd backed down from? "Rob, I really don't—"

"Good." Leaning forward, he rested his elbows on his knees. "No more of that Mr. Melbourne stuff. Friends should be on a first-name basis." His gaze became intense.

She put her hand to her throat. "We were never friends."

He frowned. "We were never enemies, were we?"

"No." She swallowed. Was it just her, or had it become suddenly warm in here? Maybe the air-conditioning wasn't working. "We were never enemies," she rasped.

He gave her that winsome smile of his, setting dragon-flies to dancing in her belly. "So there's no reason we shouldn't be friends."

Somehow she was only now realizing the space between them had lessened. Although, she wasn't sure if she'd moved closer, or if it had been him. Only a breath separated them.

Too short a distance for her peace of mind. Allowing her proximity to his handsome features. The dark ring around the iris of his eyes emphasized the vivid, sapphire hue.

If she upturned her face and he tilted his head just so…

Juliet's heart skipped a beat. Was she imagining this, or was Rob about to kiss her? Did she want him to?

"Daddy, look at me."

They both jolted and pulled back. Scrubbing his hand over his face, he turned toward his daughter. "I see you, baby."

Stopping midslide, Sophie planted her hand on her hip. "I'm not a baby, Daddy."

He held up his hand. "Sorry. Slip of the tongue. You are absolutely not a baby anymore."

The moment—whatever it was between them—had been broken.

Sophie waved him over. "Daddy."

He got to his feet.

Juliet rose also. "Rob, be care—"

He straightened, putting weight on his injured leg. But he wasn't quick enough to hide the wince. "I'm fine, Jules."

The weirdest sensation flooded her senses. No one had called her that in a long time. It had been her late Granddad Mitchell's pet name for her.

"I don't want you to hurt yourself." There was a

breathless quality to her voice. Not surprising, since she was having a hard time remembering to breathe.

"Let the doubters among us prcpare to be amazed." Crinkling his eyes, he broadened his shoulders. "I'll have you know my moonwalking skills are legendary."

"You're a legend all right." She sniffed. "In your own mind."

What had gotten into her? She sounded almost flirty.

He stared at her a second and then burst out laughing. "I had no idea you were so quick-witted. Although, I shouldn't be surprised, considering how clever you've always been."

She made an elaborate shrug. "You seem to inspire quick comebacks."

Not surprising was his effortless charm. She'd not realized how funny he actually was, though.

As a teenager, she'd hated it when people called her clever. *Clever* sounded dull and boring when she so desperately preferred *alluring* and *fascinating.* Or whatever indefinable quality the popular girls in Rob Melbourne's crowd possessed in abundance.

But coming from him, *clever* made her feel alluring and fascinating and everything else, too. Including brave.

She lifted her chin. "Let's see what you got."

He made a show of rolling his shoulders, loosening his muscles. "Only if you're sure you can handle it."

For the first time in what felt like forever—trading verbal jousts with, of all people, Rob Melbourne—she was enjoying herself.

She cocked her eyebrow. "Bring it, big shot."

Which he proceeded to do with an easy athletic grace.

"Go, Daddy, go. Go, Daddy, go," the little girl cheered.

With a self-satisfied grin, Rob continued his backward trek around the living room.

"Don't encourage him." Juliet waved her hand. "Or he'll never quit showing off."

Having proven his point, his moves became even more hilarious. Arms gliding. Feet sliding. Ballroom meets hip-hop.

Tears of laughter leaking from her eyes, she collapsed against the sofa cushions. Jumping into her lap, Sophie threw her arms around Juliet's neck. It was the nicest thing that had happened to Juliet in oh, so long.

Juliet breathed in the sweet scent of Sophie's baby shampoo. And the hint of the maple syrup she must have had for breakfast. Not to be outdone, Moose began to howl, making Sophie giggle harder.

"Stop!" Juliet held up her palm to Rob. "I beg you."

Rob dropped into the recliner, and they laughed until her sides ached.

"You're so silly, Daddy."

"Yes, he is." Juliet drew in a breath. "Wow, I had no idea how much I needed to laugh."

He swiped at his eyes. "I think we all did."

Sophie scrambled off the couch. "Does Moose have any more tricks?"

"He does." Juliet dragged herself upright and shook her head at Rob. "Where does she get the energy?"

"Children keep us young." Reaching over, he pulled his daughter into a bear hug, tickling her belly until she squealed. "And also make us old before our time."

In his eyes, she glimpsed not only the pain of the shooting last month, but perhaps of a much-longer duration. Maybe since losing his wife. It was the gaze of the survivor. Yet someone so much closer to the other side of grief than she felt herself to be.

"How did you…? I can't seem to manage to move past—" She clamped her lips shut.

But he seemed to understand what she was asking. Even if she wasn't sure what she was actually trying to say.

"Children not only get you up every morning—" he gave her a gentle smile "—they keep you on your knees, too."

Maybe that was her problem. Since Josh died, she'd had a hard time praying. Feeling most days like the cries of her heart went no further than the ceiling of her condo.

Or perhaps her problem went deeper than that. Because she had no children to get her up every morning. Nor to bend her knees to pray for.

She wasn't angry at God. At least, not after the first year. However, the bitterness had been more insidious and harder to shake.

Moose had done a lot to fill the emptiness in her heart. But as dear as the funny little dog was to her, after holding Sophie in her arms, she realized it simply couldn't compare.

The bleak grief over the loss of her child never abated. Stole her breath. Made her chest heave with repressed tears.

As a distraction, she scooped Moose into her arms, a barrier against the despair. Scrabbling higher in her grip, Moose's tongue darted out and licked her neck. Somehow, Moose knew. He always knew when she was feeling low.

"I also think grief is a journey." Rob sighed. "And it takes as long as it takes."

She avoided his too-penetrating stare. "Next trick." She set Moose on the ground.

Keeping her feet apart, she began walking across the length of the room. "Weave. And weave. And weave."

Moose darted between her legs, doing a figure eight around her strides.

"Hurray!" Sophie fist-pumped the air. "Hurray for Moose."

Juliet lavished some love on her sweet companion. Hurray for Moose indeed.

Glancing at the clock on the kitchen wall, she couldn't believe she and Moose had already been here a couple of hours.

"We should probably go."

"Aww!" Sophie moaned. "Does she have to?"

Rob pressed his hands on the armrests of the recliner to rise.

"Please." Hastening over, she put her hand on his shoulder. "Don't get up."

"Stay with us, Juliet," he rasped.

Her breath hitched.

Rob covered her hand on his shoulder with his. "Stay for lunch."

The low humming throb of a headache formed at her temples. "I… I can't." Snatching her hand free, she back-pedaled in a decidedly un-moonwalk fashion. "Moose needs a break."

He stood up. "Juliet…"

"For exercise. A potty break. To go off duty. Time to just be a normal dog." She was babbling again.

The walls were closing in. She hadn't had an anxiety attack in three years. Not since Moose came into her life.

"Also… I… I have errands to run. Can't stay for lunch."

Or anything else. Most especially not for whatever it was that thrummed between her and Rob.

Juliet grabbed the backpack. "We can do an afternoon session at three o'clock if that works for you."

Sophie tugged at her father's shirttail. "What's a session, Daddy?"

Why had she said *session*? She never said that to a child. No one, not even a four-year-old, wanted to feel like a case or a project.

His eyes narrowed. "Three will work for us. Not like we're going anywhere."

Sophie's brow creased. "What's a session, Miss Juliet?"

Momentarily quelling her frantic desire to flee, she touched the little girl's soft cheek. "I meant playdate. Moose and I will be back at three o'clock to play."

Sophie gave her a hug, sunshine beaming in her smile.

Feeling like the coward she was, Juliet beat a hasty retreat. Heart thudding, she put Moose into the car and threw herself behind the wheel. She hadn't been lying. She did have errands to run.

Like tracking down Rob's Aunt Evelyn and getting to the bottom of what was going on with Juliet's mom.

Right. Juliet cranked the engine. That's exactly why she'd run from Rob's house like the clock was tolling midnight.

Cinderella she was not. And Rob Melbourne was most definitely not her Prince Charming.

She'd buried her handsome prince in a grave in Greensboro. No fairy-tale ending for her. And happily-ever-afters only happened once in a lifetime.

Didn't they?

Chapter Four

After lunch, Sophie colored in her princess book at the kitchen table, and Rob went to answer the door off the back screened porch. The friends and family entrance.

His best friend and Laurel Grove paramedic, Trace Burton, held up a white paper bag. "Coffee?"

Grinning, Rob threw open the door. "I hope you brought more than coffee."

Having just finished his shift and still wearing his uniform, Trace shouldered his way inside. "I brought doughnuts, too." He set the bag on the table inside the screened porch.

Rob pulled out one of the chairs. "I appreciate you keeping me supplied with pastries while I'm on leave from the Greensboro PD."

Sitting down, he reached for the bag. He set one coffee cup in front of his best friend and took another for himself.

Trace plopped into the chair. "A guy needs to look out for his buddies. Even if it is end-of-the-day, didn't-sell doughnuts."

Rob propped his leg on a small stool. He'd never admit it, but the moonwalk thing hadn't been the best idea for a guy recovering from a bullet wound to the thigh. But the last thing he'd wanted was to appear weak in front of Juliet.

He took the lid off the coffee cup. Steam curled above the brew. He took an appreciative sip. "Ahhhh. I needed that."

End-of-the-day doughnuts became just fine when dunked in a cup of hot coffee.

Trace leaned back against the chair. "Where's Doodlebug?"

Rob motioned toward the interior door he'd left open so he could keep an eye on Sophie. And vice versa.

Trace craned his neck to get a better look inside the house. "Hey, Doodlebug!" He waved.

"I'm not a doodlebug, Uncle Trace." Bent over her coloring book, Sophie made a face. "I'm a girl."

"Oh, yeah," Trace called. "Thanks for reminding me."

She gave him a look-what-I-have-to-deal-with sort of glance. Not unlike the look Aunt Evie used to give Rob when he and Trace were teenagers up to their usual antics.

Unrepentant, Trace grinned at the little girl. "Call 'em like I see 'em, Doodlebug."

She pointed a red crayon in their direction. "You and Daddy are so silly."

Trace laughed. "Your father's been a bad influence on me since high school. I'd have been class valedictorian if not for him."

Rob rolled his eyes. "More like class clown, and you can't blame me for that."

Ignoring them, Sophie returned to her crayon creation. Trace grabbed one of the glazed doughnuts. There were lines of weariness etched around his mouth.

"Hard shift?"

Like the firefighters, the paramedics worked twenty-four-hour shifts.

Trace shrugged. "Nothing too dramatic. I work in boring old Laurel Grove, remember? I leave the tough cases to you big-city detectives." He took a bite of the doughnut.

Rob grimaced. "From where I'm sitting—" he motioned toward his leg "—Laurel Grove is looking pretty good."

Trace chewed and swallowed. "It's been great the last few weeks unwinding from my shift with you and Doodlebug before heading home to crash." He winked at Rob. "Except for the wound that grounded you in the first place, of course."

Rob snagged his favorite cruller. "Except for that. I didn't even get it in the line of duty."

With their sometimes-conflicting schedules, he and Trace weren't able to get together often, outside the occasional weekend fishing excursion to Uncle Adrian's well-stocked farm pond.

Trace leaned forward, elbows propped on the wooden table. "Never met a cop that didn't feel on duty twenty-four seven if the situation demanded it."

Rob sighed. "It's in the oath."

"A calling." Trace wrapped his hands around his cup. "I get that. It's in the blood."

"Same for you guys."

If Trace or any other paramedic had been on scene that day, they'd have been running toward the injured, too, not thinking of their own safety. A first responder's dedication to serve and protect.

Rob's gaze flickered through the open door to the kitchen. "I just wish she hadn't been there. To see me get…you know." He bit his lip.

Trace shoved another doughnut at him. "She's tough like her dad. Kids are resilient. She'll bounce back. Especially now you've got that Paw Pals person working with you."

Rob raised his cup. "Funny you should mention our class valedictorian…" He filled his friend in on their initial visit with Juliet and Moose that morning. "She and that ridiculous dog of hers will be back at three." He took a quick peek at his cell, lying on the table. Didn't want time to get away from him.

Although, it wasn't like he had much else going on. He smiled, recalling Moose's tricks. Juliet was becoming the highlight of his day. For more than one reason. His smile fled.

Trace blinked at him. "Here I was imagining some retired lady volunteer coming with her dog, and you get someone our age we've known most of our lives. What a coincidence."

Rob looked at him over the rim of the cup. "You know how law enforcement feels about coincidence."

"Knowing you, you're seeing God's hand at work, I guess. For what purpose do you suppose?"

He glanced at his lanky friend. Due to his rocky childhood, Trace struggled with faith. Who didn't in the kind of work they did?

"This is about my daughter. Nothing else." He narrowed his eyes at his pal. "But I couldn't believe how Soph—" he lowered his voice "—how You-Know-Who took to her and the dog."

Trace slurped down a swallow of coffee. "After this, You-Know-Who is going to want a dog of her own. You know that, right?" He gave Rob a slightly wicked grin. "Maybe even a mom."

"Don't you start," he growled.

Watching Juliet with his little girl had been an eye-opener. She'd been so tender and loving. And how Sophie had responded to her had proven equally revealing.

His heart had ached, realizing what Sophie had missed in not having a mom. Aunt Evie and those nosy Knit-Knack friends of hers had been after him for over a year to wade back into the dating pool again. But he'd resisted, not yet ready to let go of what he'd shared with Katrina. Not willing to share Sophie, either.

But for the first time, he wondered what it would be like to have someone in his life again. Someone like Juliet?

These emotions were new and confusing. Not something he was ready to admit out loud.

"So." Trace sprawled in the chair. "Juliet Mitchell's all grown-up. If she's anything like her mom, I'm imagining she's a looker. Is she available for someone as extraordinarily good-looking as me?"

Annoyance at his still-single buddy—and some other, unfamiliar emotion—needled Rob. "She's Juliet Newkirk now."

Trace's goofy face fell. "Aw. She's married."

"No…" He gritted his teeth. "She's a widow."

"Like you." Trace smirked. "I see where this wind is blowing. She's off-limits. Or should I say, paws-off." He did an exaggerated wink-wink. "Get it, *paws-off*?" He laughed at his own joke.

"Juliet's not like me. And she's not… *I'm* not… *We're* not…"

Trace chuckled. "Thanks for the crystal clear clarification. She must be something else to have our silver-tongued lad stumbling for words."

Juliet Newkirk was something else. The attraction he'd felt toward her had little to do with her appearance. The instant spark between them had taken him by surprise. And disturbed him more than a little.

It had been just him and Sophie for so long. He was happy with that, completely content with the current state of his life. Wasn't he?

Sure, he got lonely after he put Sophie to bed at night. Since Katrina's death, it was the ordinary joys of sharing a life with someone he found himself actually missing the most.

A quick kiss before heading out to work. Discussing their respective days over dinner. Dreaming about future plans together.

Things he'd taken for granted until Katrina died. He'd miss her until the day he died, but the sharp, gut-twisting pain of her loss had blunted over time. And for some inexplicable reason, he'd found himself hungering once again for the simple joys of a shared life.

He exhaled. "Don't you have somewhere to be, dude? Like putting your head on a pillow? Getting those forty winks."

"You're probably right." Trace polished his knuckles on his white uniform shirt. "This kind of handsome doesn't happen by accident."

Rob nearly choked on a swig of coffee. "Please don't let me stand in the way of your much-needed beauty sleep—emphasis on *much*."

Trace laughed. "Good to see you, too, bro. Bye, Doodlebug," he hollered into the kitchen.

From the kitchen, a child-sized groan.

"I think my work here is done for the day." Trace stood up, scraping the chair across the concrete floor. "Although, I've half a mind to stick around and reintroduce Juliet to this prime hunk of manhood." Trace pounded his chest with his hand.

Rising more slowly, Rob shook his head. "Go already."

Trace shrugged. "I'm going, I'm going. No need to be rude. What would Aunt Evie say about such behavior?"

Rob pushed at his shoulder. "I'll tell you what I'm going to say if you don't hit the road."

"You wound me, dude." Trace put a hand to his chest again. "Some friend you are to keep the lovely Juliet to yourself. But I'd still love to meet this pooch of hers." He cocked his head. "I find myself hankering for a canine friend of my own."

Rob made a sarcastic comment—not so under his breath—about what Trace could do with his suddenly discovered affinity for dogs.

Trace laughed all the way around the house to his truck.

Rob couldn't help but grin after him. Trace had stuck by Rob through thick and thin. A stalwart friend who'd allowed Rob to take out his anger and work through his grief after losing Katrina.

Friends like that were priceless. And exceedingly rare.

Trace was also right that the unexpected upside of Rob's injury meant more time to spend with friends and family. It was one of the reasons he moved home two years ago after Katrina's death.

He'd transferred from his old job with the police force in Raleigh, where they'd lived after getting married, straight into the Homicide squad in the Greensboro Criminal Investigations Division with relative ease.

But the biggest reason of all? He'd needed a change in scenery from the constant reminders of Katrina's death. To continue his career and make the commute each day to Greensboro, he relied upon the support of Aunt Evie and Uncle Adrian to watch over then-two-year-old Sophie.

As for keeping Juliet to himself? He wasn't sure why

he felt so protective—if *protective* was the right word—
over Moose's feisty owner. Trace Burton wasn't without
a certain self-deprecating charm of his own.

When it came to Juliet, was he jealous?

Frowning, he tightened his jaw. Absolutely not. They
barely knew each other. They'd just met.

Not exactly true. More like reacquainted. But he wasn't
the same person he'd been in high school and neither
was she.

He stuffed the napkins into the paper bag and loped
into the kitchen.

Blue crayon poised midair, Sophie surveyed the
scrunched bag in his hand. "Did Uncle Trace bring me
a doughnut?"

"Doesn't he always?" Rob set the last doughnut in
front of her. "Pink icing with sprinkles as usual."

Sophie batted her eyes at him. "Pink is my favorite
color."

He made a show of shuddering. "So girlie."

She pursed her small lips. "I am a girl, Daddy."

He kissed the top of her head. "Don't I know it?"
Lord, help me.

At this rate, how was he ever going to handle the teen
years on his own? "Want a sip of my coffee?" he teased.

She made the little clicking noise she did with her
tongue against her teeth when she was disgusted. "Coffee makes you ugly, Daddy."

"Right you are, Sophie." He smiled at this oft-repeated
exchange between them. "You make sure you stay away
from coffee and those froggy boys. They'll make you
ugly, too."

"Oh, Daddy…" She turned back to her coloring book.
"Boys aren't frogs."

Maybe not, but he already knew none of them would

ever be good enough for his girl. He'd need a different, less subjective perspective when she was old enough to date. His stomach clenched at the mere thought of Sophie dating.

"It's almost time for Miss Juliet and Moose, isn't it, Daddy?"

His gaze flitted to the clock above the sink. "Soon."

"I need to finish this page so I can show Miss Juliet."

He ruffled her hair, making her squeal.

"You're messing up my hair, Daddy!"

But it was worth it to hear Sophie sound more like herself. More like the Sophie he'd feared lost forever on that day four weeks ago.

After subduing the shooter, he'd returned to where he'd hidden Sophie to keep her safe during the rampage. She'd been crying, but when she saw the blood on his pant leg, she'd gone quiet. She'd gotten quieter and quieter every day since. Until Juliet and Moose showed up.

"I'll watch for them. You finish your coloring."

Restless, he moved to the living room.

"You'll stay where I can see you?" Her voice trembled.

Guilt struck him anew. Leaving her while he stopped the shooter had traumatized her. This was all his fault.

"I'll be here." He swallowed. "Right where you can see me."

Leg aching again, he leaned against the front window overlooking the street and twitched aside the curtain.

He wasn't sure what to make of Juliet. They'd been getting along so well until they weren't. He didn't understand what had happened. What he'd said or done to rattle her.

She confused him. First, she blew hot, then cold. He didn't get her. Juliet was unlike anyone he'd ever known.

Which was both bad and good. Bad, because she made

him want to tear out his hair. And good, because she made him feel something he never expected to feel again after Katrina's death.

Yet earlier, she'd practically run out of his house. She was obviously still going through a rough time over the loss of her husband. Not looking for anything other than friendship.

Better for him to know now at this stage in their relationship.

As if they actually had a relationship outside Sophie's sessions. He clenched his jaw. That's all he and his child were to her. A job. Rightly so, he supposed.

He and Juliet didn't really know each other. No matter how much he'd like to rectify that. An admission that continued to floor him.

But there'd been no getting her out of his mind. He'd tossed and turned last night, thinking of the dark-haired dog handler.

He wasn't sure what it was that drew him to her. She was a woman still very much in love with her dead husband. And he… He was what?

Rob ran his hand over his face. Based on Sophie's response to Juliet, he was a man in sore need of providing his daughter with a mother. He'd never considered dating since Katrina died. What had changed?

Juliet Newkirk had walked into his life, that's what.

But he needed to excise any feelings she stirred within him. He'd told Trace the truth. This Paw Pals therapy thing was about Sophie.

And only about Sophie. That's all it could ever be. Because he didn't have the emotional bandwidth or courage for anything else.

Chapter Five

At the Gilmer farm, Juliet had just gotten Moose out of the car when Rob's uncle Adrian came out of the red barn. He was a tall, big-boned, silver-haired man.

His weather-beaten features broke into a smile. He opened his arms and she went into them. He'd taught her so much not only about animals through 4-H, but about life, too.

"So good to see you, baby doll."

Tears smarted her eyes. Only Mr. Adrian called her that. With a final, quick squeeze, he released her.

"Let me get a gander at you." The lines crinkling from the corner of his hazel eyes lifted and fanned out. "Pretty as a picture. Evelyn tells me you're doing wonderful things."

Not a word of recrimination for how she'd neglected him over the last few years. Guilt washed over her. Two years ago, he'd suffered a heart attack. It had been touch-and-go for a while. Even then, she hadn't found the heart or the courage to come home.

"I'm sorry I wasn't here for you, Mr. Adrian."

"Hush now." He waved his meaty hand, as if to banish her words. "You've had your business to establish."

He gave her a wink. "I like to think I taught you a lot of what you needed to know to run one."

It was true. He'd mentored the skinny, awkward city girl through the process of hand-raising a calf. Taught her how to weigh the cost of running a food animal enterprise. And comforted her after the state fair, when JoJo was sold as intended at auction.

Juliet's mouth trembled. "I... I just couldn't face the possibility of one more loss, Mr. Adrian."

"You did what you had to do." He gave her a rueful smile. "Just like with JoJo. Love. Loss. Letting go. The lessons of a lifetime we're all still in the process of learning. I'm fine now. And better yet, you're here. That's what matters."

She hugged him again. His strong arms went around her. Her father had deserted her pregnant mother. She'd never known him. Mr. Adrian was as close to a father figure as she'd come.

He'd always made her feel loved, cherished and safe, how she imagined the best fathers made their children feel.

Something niggled at the edges of her mind. Had something else happened between Rob and Sophie on the day of the shooting?

But Moose yipped, distracting her. Reminding them he was there, too. On the off chance anyone could possibly forget about him. She smiled at her sweet, tiny dog.

Mr. Adrian grinned. "Well, if it isn't my old friend Moose. What a day for reunions."

Bending, the sixtyish farmer gave Moose a vigorous head rubbing. Moose made cute little noises. Showing his love, he licked the farmer's chin. Mr. Adrian laughed.

Moose did the prancing, quivery dance he did when he was happy.

Strawberry fields stretched to the tree line. Up and down the rows, clusters of people with white buckets leaned over the plants.

Juliet breathed deeply. The scent of strawberries perfumed the air. It was her favorite season at Gilmer Farm. "Doesn't look like much has changed."

One of the reasons she loved this place so much. In a world where change was often a constant, it was a blessing to have the farm and these good people in her life.

Juliet imagined Rob must feel the same. Especially when he'd found himself widowed so young with a small toddler to raise alone. No wonder he'd come home to Laurel Grove.

So why hadn't she?

Juliet swallowed. Her default answer when anyone dared to ask was the need to remain in Greensboro for her business. But if Rob could make commuting into the city work, why hadn't she?

Because returning to Laurel Grove would mean finally accepting her old life with Josh was over?

"How about I take Moose for a tour of the property?" Adrian reached for the leash. "I'm sure you'd like to visit a spell with Evelyn. She's in the middle of jam making."

Juliet handed him the leash. "Of course, she is. It's May. How's the pick-your-own business this year?"

"Best crop ever."

She smiled. "You say that every year."

"But it's true." He grinned. "The Lord is good. Every year, His goodness to me only gets better and better."

Therein lay the difference between her and Mr. Adrian. No matter the hardship, his faith was as solid and reliable as the man himself.

"Make sure you take a bucket home to your ma, and

jam, too. My woman makes entirely too much of that stuff for an old man like me to eat by myself."

"Thank you. I know Mom will appreciate it." She touched his arm. "And you're not old."

He motioned her toward the sturdy, white farmhouse with the silver tin roof under the clear blue Carolina sky. "While you're at it, Sophie loves strawberries. When you head over to his place later, bring her and Rob a bucket."

She planted her hands on her hips. "Does everybody in the county know my schedule?"

He moved away. "No, of course not." Moose trotted alongside him. "Only folks in Laurel Grove." His laughter floated behind him as he headed toward the barn.

She strolled onto the wraparound porch and pulled open the door. "Knock, knock?" she called inside the house.

"Juliet?" Evelyn poked her head around the door frame leading to the kitchen. Wiping her hands on a dish towel, she smiled. "What a nice surprise. Have you had lunch yet?"

"I stopped by the house and grabbed a sandwich, but thanks anyway."

She'd taken Moose to her mom's and let him run to his heart's content in the fenced backyard.

"You mean to tell me you ate lunch alone?" Evelyn's eyebrow arched. "Why didn't you eat with Rob and Sophie?"

Because she couldn't trust herself to hold in the slightly disconcerting, totally perplexing feelings for Evelyn's nephew a second longer than she had to.

Juliet gave her a thin smile. "I eat by myself every day, Miss Evelyn."

"All by your lonesome…" Evelyn tsked.

"I'm not lonesome." She tried not to grit her teeth. "I have Moose."

From the look Evelyn shot her, it was clear her mom's best friend didn't believe her.

"Whatever you say, sweetie." The older woman tugged her into the kitchen. "How about joining me for dessert?"

The window over the sink was open. Several strawberry pies sat cooling on the sill. The aromas wafting through the bright, cheery kitchen were not to be ignored.

She did a quick check of the clock on the stove. Plenty of time before her afternoon appointment with Sophie.

Evelyn pulled one of the pies onto the countertop. "A slice of pie?"

She gave in without too much resistance. "Sure." She had a few questions to put to the older lady about her mom.

"How about a scoop of vanilla ice cream on top?"

Better wrap this case up fast. The longer she stayed in Laurel Grove, the bigger likelihood her waistline would expand. "Yes, ma'am."

Evelyn's Melbourne blue eyes twinkled. "I just finished making iced strawberry tea. How about a glass?"

Smiling, Juliet nodded. Southern women loved to feed their favorite people. It was how they showed their love.

Juliet sat down at the scrubbed clean farm table. Like ruby-red jewels, tiny jars of strawberry jam gleamed from the apple-green work surface of the vintage Hoosier cabinet.

Evelyn placed the plate with the scoop of melting ice cream dribbling across the pie in front of her. Juliet bit back an inward sigh. Southern women also loved giving big helpings.

Taking the opposite chair, Evelyn waited for her taste test. "How is it?"

She dug into the pie and took a bite. Delicious flavors danced on her tongue. "As good as I remembered."

Worth every calorie. As long as she didn't make a habit of it. Juliet finished her pie while Evelyn caught her up on farm happenings.

As Evelyn chatted about the new anthem she was working on with the church choir, Juliet couldn't help but recall how Adrian and Evelyn had taken in Rob after his parents were killed in an automobile accident. The farm was a wonderful place to grow up. They loved Rob like a son. And were devoted to Sophie, too.

She laid down her fork. "At the Ewe, something you said made me wonder if there was something going on with my mom."

Evelyn steepled her hands on the table. "Your mother is my best friend in the world. If she hasn't said anything to you, then it's not my place to tell her secrets."

"Secrets?" Juliet gaped at her. "What's going on? Has something happened?" Her gaze skittered around the kitchen before landing on Evelyn's knitting bag in the corner alcove. "Is it the store? She's poured her life into that place."

"She's poured her life into you. It's true she's put her life savings into the store." Evelyn laced her hands together. "But the Ewe is doing well."

Panic ricocheted in her chest like a silver ball in a pinball machine. "So it's something to do with her health? Is that what you're saying?"

The older woman bit her lip.

"Miss Evelyn, please."

The older lady tilted her head. "Have you noticed anything different about her lately?"

"I don't know." Juliet threw out her hands. "She

seemed a bit fragile when I hugged her. Like she might break." Her mind raced. "Is my mom sick?"

The older woman avoided her gaze.

"Please don't make me play twenty questions, Miss Evelyn."

Evelyn raised her chin. "Since your grandfather died, your mother has been very alone, Juliet."

"I know." Remorse stabbed at her heart. "And I'm sorry. But as I told my mom the other day, I'm in a better place now."

"Are you?"

She ignored the soft-spoken rejoinder. "I'm here for her."

Evelyn's gaze bored into her. "Do you mean physically or just emotionally?"

She stiffened. "Is this some not-so-subtle attempt to get me to move back to Laurel Grove?"

Reaching across the table, Evelyn patted her hand. "No, sweetie." Her eyes shone with a glimmer of tears. As if what she was about to say would hurt her as much as Juliet.

"This is about me sticking my neck out at the risk of offending you and alienating your mother. To remind you that you are not the only one who has experienced pain and suffering."

Sucking in a breath, Juliet drew back, laying her hand in her lap. "I wasn't aware there was an expiration date to grief."

Evelyn bit her lip.

"What about the children Moose and I help at the hospital?" She sounded defensive, but couldn't help herself.

Evelyn gave her a small smile. "And if Paw Pals receives the grant, so many more will be helped throughout the greater Triad area."

Which took the starch out of her spine. Yet was there any truth to what Evelyn said? That she'd only been thinking about herself and her own pain for far too long? Everything within her wanted to deny Evelyn's gentle rebuke. But a sinking feeling seized her gut, whispering it was true.

She swiped at her eyes. Evelyn reached for her hand again and this time, Juliet let her take it.

"What should I do about my mom, Miss Evelyn?"

"I cannot betray the confidence Lesley has placed in me, but…"

Juliet held her breath.

"She's made quite a few trips to Greensboro over the last month."

"You mean in addition to when I've seen her?"

Evelyn inclined her head. "There may even be another trip planned for this week."

"Like an appointment?"

Evelyn fluttered her lashes. "You didn't hear the word *appointment* from me."

"But how would— The calendar. The one that hangs inside the pantry door."

Evelyn gave a slow nod.

"When I was a little girl, Mom would always write important appointments on that calendar."

Evelyn's lips twitched. "And at our age, I assure you we're not apt to change the habits of a lifetime. I think if you ask her, she'll tell you what's really been going on in her life for the past six weeks."

Juliet winced. "That long?"

She felt like the most clueless, worst daughter on the planet for not picking up on her mom's distress.

"Why didn't she tell me, Miss Evelyn?"

"Lesley's been on her own since before you were born."

It had been the unexpected pregnancy that had brought Juliet's then-college-aged mom home for a reconciliation with her estranged father.

Juliet shook her head. "But despite living in Greensboro, I always believed Mom and I were close in the ways that mattered."

Evelyn squeezed her hand. "And you are. But Lesley is adamant about not becoming a burden—"

"Mom would never be a burden."

"In light of what you've been going through since your husband passed, she didn't want to add to your troubles."

Juliet had kept friends and family, including her precious mother, at an emotional arm's length since Josh died. If her mom didn't feel she could or should confide in her, Juliet had no one to blame but herself.

She took a deep breath. "I promise you, Miss Evelyn, I will do everything in my power to reassure Mom I'm present for her." She lifted her chin. "Both physically and emotionally. Whatever it takes. She's not alone. She has me."

Evelyn sat back in the chair. "You and the Lord. That's all she's ever needed. Thank you, sweetie."

With a swift glance at the clock, Juliet rose. "Thank you for the kick in the pants about Mom."

Evelyn jumped up. "Let me get you some strawberries and jam to take to your mom."

Her mother's best friend bustled around the kitchen, transferring a large colander of washed strawberries into a plastic container and boxing the other pie. "You should have time to drop them off at the house before your next visit with Sophie at three."

Juliet threw out her hands. "The Laurel Grove grapevine strikes again."

"Not the grapevine this time. Haven't you heard? We've

got all the modern conveniences now." Evelyn's eyes twinkled. "Indoor plumbing *and* cell phones. Laurel Grove's gone totally twenty-first century."

Juliet laughed.

"Rob called me after you left, with an update." Evelyn tucked everything into a canvas bag and handed her the pie. "You'd save me a trip if you'd deliver a pie and some jam to Rob, too. That boy does love my strawberry pie."

Suddenly nervous, she shouldered the bag and clutched the box of pie. "How does he think it's going?"

"He's amazed at how quickly Sophie has bonded with Moose. And you." Evelyn gave her a wistful smile. "I've done my best, but I think it's obvious how much Sophie has missed having a motherly presence in her life. You've been good for Rob, too."

Juliet backed toward the door. Among their various charity endeavors, the Knit-Knackers were also renowned for their matchmaking. "We're friends, Miss Evelyn."

"All the better." Evelyn had a mischievous gleam in her eyes Juliet didn't like. "Can't ever have too many friends." She winked at her.

Turning on her heel, she called her thanks and fled. Getting out of there while she still could, unscathed.

But she had a sneaking suspicion the more time she spent with Rob and his adorable little girl, emerging unscathed might become increasingly less likely.

Rob opened the door.

Leash wrapped around her hand, Juliet held up a brown canvas bag. "I come bearing gifts."

He grinned and stepped aside. "You've been to Aunt Evie's. Is that pie I smell?" He sniffed the air appreciatively.

She tilted her head. "Strawberry pie is a favorite of yours, I believe."

He motioned her toward the kitchen. "Blueberry, peach or cherry, too. I'm an equal opportunity pie-eater."

Moose strutted in with her.

She threw Rob a hesitant smile. "Good to know."

Was bringing him the pie an apology of sorts for how things had gotten tense before? He'd made a career out of his ability to read situations and people. It'd saved his life more than once.

But with Juliet, it was hard to tell what she was thinking. She held her feelings close. What would happen if she ever stopped bottling her emotions? If her emotional geyser ever erupted, something within him wanted to be the one to help her put herself back together.

The little dog yipped to get Rob's attention.

He patted the small fur ball's head. "Hello to you, too, Moose."

Whining, Moose strained toward the living room and the toy corner Rob had set up.

She set the bag on the counter. "Where's my favorite four-year-old?"

Her words did a lot to restore his faith in her. After what had felt like a rebuff earlier that morning, he wasn't sure where Juliet's head was regarding his daughter.

Sophie poked her head around the couch. "Miss Juliet, can you and Moose come play with me?"

Juliet glanced at him.

He shrugged. "I'd hoped she might have fallen asleep. She's droopy. I'm not sure how the afternoon will go."

Moose barked an excited greeting.

"Hey, Moosie-Moose." Sophie's face brightened. "Hey, boy."

Rob smiled. "Maybe they'll play so hard, Moose will wear Sophie out and we'll get a decent night's sleep."

Juliet unclipped the little dog and he took off toward Sophie.

Crouching, his daughter greeted the butterfly-eared dog as if they'd been parted for weeks and not hours. And Moose acted as if he'd just been reunited with his dearest friend.

He winced as Moose licked both sides of her face, but it only made Sophie giggle.

"Miss Juliet, will you come look at my dollhouse, too?" Sophie called.

"I'm going to help your dad unpack the goodies your aunt Evie sent." She threw him a glance. "I'll be there in a sec."

Sophie and Moose made for the toys.

Thanks to the open floor plan, they were able to keep an eye on the dog and Sophie.

He watched his daughter take out the furnishings of her dollhouse to show to Moose one by one. Then he turned to Juliet. "I've been wanting a chance to talk about your initial assessment and where we go from here."

"This morning, I wanted to get Sophie acquainted with Moose and help her relax." Juliet handed him the jam and the boxed pie to put away. "But now that I've had time to interact with her, I have some thoughts about how we should proceed."

He slumped against the counter. "I'm ready to try anything that will help."

"It's called exposure therapy."

Opening a cabinet, he set the jam jar on a shelf. "What does that involve?"

"We naturally avoid things that provoke anxiety. People think by avoiding triggers to our fears, we become stronger."

He frowned. "But actually, the opposite occurs, right?"

"Exactly." She moved closer to him, and he caught a whiff of something floral. "It's in confronting our fears in a gradual, controlled setting that allows us to overcome the anxiety. The hospital counselor believes Sophie's suffering from agoraphobia, resulting from the traumatic shooter event."

Pain lanced his heart. How had this happened to his sweet Sophie?

He raked his hand over his face. "It seems so hopeless."

"It's not hopeless. We just have to break the association in her mind." She gestured at the window. "That everything out there is unsafe."

He shifted, taking the pressure off his leg. "From what I see daily in my profession, I might beg to differ."

"I wonder..." Juliet's brow scrunched.

He stiffened. "You wonder how much my work plays into the fears tearing my little girl apart right now? Don't think I don't."

"Let's take one thing at a time. I'm hoping Moose's presence will help her talk about her fears. Sometimes getting someone to articulate what's frightening them is huge."

He crossed his arms. "Suppose she starts to feel panicked?"

"We're going to take things step-by-step. I'll teach her breathing techniques to help Sophie self-regulate her emotions when she begins to feel out of control."

He tightened his jaw. "I don't know if I'm going to be able to stand by and watch her struggle."

"I promise not to push more than she can handle."

Juliet looked at him. "I have to warn you, though. The natural response when you see your child in distress is to jump in and make it better. Yet in the long run it makes it harder for Sophie to calm herself. We're going to give her lots of practice to build her confidence in coping with stressful situations. She won't always have Dad around in every situation to make her feel better."

His gut twisted. Thanks to his overly developed rescuer complex, Sophie hadn't had her father the one time she needed him most.

Rob clenched his fists. "If only we hadn't gone to buy a birthday gift at that store on that particular day."

"The if-onlys and what-ifs will destroy you, Rob."

"You sound as if you speak from experience."

She wouldn't meet his gaze. "Guilt is never a productive use of time."

"It feels so overwhelming. And sitting around waiting for a breakthrough has never been my style."

"You've done exactly as the trauma counselor advised. You've done everything right thus far."

He grimaced. "Except for putting her in danger in the first place."

"You can't keep thinking like that." She shook her head. "Children pick up on our anxieties and fears. Since the incident, she's looked to you for security, which you've been quick to provide. You've stuck with family routines around meals and bedtimes. Reassuring Sophie that life will be okay again."

"You think so?" He swallowed. "Katrina was always so much more intuitive about parenting than I was. I'm never sure if I'm doing the best thing for Sophie."

She touched his sleeve. "You need to stop beating yourself up. We're going to find a way to help Sophie get past what happened."

"Thanks for the pep talk, Coach. I needed that." He made a wry face. "Maybe as much as Sophie. It's hard parenting alone."

For a split second, compassion and something inscrutable glimmered in her dark eyes. "You're doing a great job with Sophie." She play-punched his bicep. "Which comes as no surprise. Has there ever been anything you didn't do well once you set your mind to it?"

"Never mastered calculus." He gave her a shaky laugh. "So what's the plan?"

She sighed. "Once I get her to open up, with her input, we'll put together a plan with reasonable goals to help her feel braver."

"Just getting her out to the porch would be remarkable."

"And very achievable. Have patience."

He extended his hand. "We're in this together?"

She grasped his hand. "For the long haul."

Her hand was warm. There was an unexpected strength in her long, slender fingers.

"Thanks, Juliet. For everything you're doing for my child."

After this morning's tension, he wanted to reassure Juliet of their professional relationship.

Getting back his daughter depended on Juliet's expertise. And no matter that his confused heart urged him to seek more, Sophie had to come first.

Chapter Six

Later that afternoon, Juliet took a slow turn around Sophie's bedroom.

"Sophie…" Juliet put her finger to her chin and appeared to give the matter serious thought. "Would your favorite color happen to be…pink?"

The little girl clasped her hands together. "It is. It is. It is." Reacting to the excitement in her voice, Moose did an exuberant prance around them.

"What was your first clue?" Arms folded, Rob smirked. "The pink iron bed? The pink lampshade? Or the shaggy pink rug?"

"Don't forget the pink-striped valances and white bedspread with the small pink butterflies."

Sophie plopped onto the bed. "I love butterflies."

Juliet's mouth quirked. "Who doesn't?"

A trail of 3D, washi tape butterflies streamed across the wall next to the headboard.

"I've never seen anything like this before."

"An ongoing craft project of Aunt Evie's and Sophie's." Hands on his hips, Rob surveyed the space. "The entire room is the joint design genius of those two."

Juliet smiled. "I love it."

The effect was one of movement, joy and life. The white shelves contained well-loved dolls and stuffed animals. The appealing color scheme captured Sophie's bubbly personality.

Or, at least the child she'd been before the incident. The child Juliet was determined to see restored to wholeness.

Sophie took hold of her hand. "Would you like to make butterflies with me, Miss Juliet?"

"I'd love to."

Sophie had an entire tub of colorful washi tapes. She and Juliet sat at the kitchen table with scissors and cardstock butterfly templates.

Rob moved toward the screened porch.

Scissors in hand, Juliet paused. "Aren't you going to make butterflies, too, Rob?"

"I think you two have got the craft project under control." He smiled. "I'll be out here doing my PT exercises if you need me."

Moose swaggered over to him. Rob threw her a glance. She shrugged. "Maybe butterflies aren't his thing, either."

Laughing, Rob moved out to the porch. Fluffy tail swishing, Moose followed on his heels.

The small dog with the big heart always knew who needed him the most and when. She had a feeling the little canine with the butterfly ears was growing on the police detective. The Moose Effect never failed.

She turned her attention to cutting strips of tape. Sophie's job was to randomly layer the tape on the butterfly-shaped cardstock for a variegated effect.

"This is a fun." She handed Sophie a four-inch strip. "Aunt Evie's idea?"

Her tongue sticking out from her teeth, Sophie nodded, carefully applying the sticky tape just so.

It was a cute idea and very creative. The Knit-Knackers were a creative, if sometimes meddling, bunch. Although in her mother's case, she was glad Evelyn had gotten Juliet involved.

She continued to hand the strips to Sophie. This might prove a great activity to get the little girl to open up about her fears. "What do you know about butterflies, Sophie?"

"I know a bunch." Sophie looked up. "My class visited a butterfly farm."

Juliet recalled from the file that Sophie attended a preschool program.

Sophie's blue eyes clouded. "I don't go to school anymore."

"Do you miss going to school?"

The child's gaze flicked to the window and the world beyond before darting to the door off the screened porch. "I miss my friends, but I can't leave Daddy. It's not safe."

They worked in silence for a few moments.

"When I was a little girl, I couldn't say *butterfly*, so I called them flutterbies."

Sophie grinned. "That's so silly, Miss Juliet. I can say *butterfly*. You must have been so little. Littler than me."

"Oh, I was. Not a big girl like you." Juliet handed her a piece of tape. "One thing I loved about the flutterbies…"

Sophie giggled.

"I loved how they floated from flower to flower. Flitting through the air. Catching the wind." She demonstrated with her hands, replicating the flitter-flutter of their wings. "So free. So beautiful. Soaring in the sky."

"Show me, Miss Juliet. I want to soar like the flutterbies." Sophie gave her an impish grin. "I said that wrong on purpose. So you wouldn't feel bad about being so little back then."

Juliet hugged her. Sophie had such a sweet, caring

heart. "I appreciate that, darling." Juliet showed her how to lace her fingers together.

The little girl flittered about, dancing around the kitchen island.

"You know it's not easy for butterflies. They don't start out being beautiful, winged creatures."

Sophie slipped back into her chair. "They start out as caterpillars. I remember." She made a face. "Not so pretty."

"But the important thing is they grow and don't stay that way."

"I have a book about a caterpillar. I'll show you." Sophie raced over to a basket of books beside the sofa.

Returning, she flipped the pages. "There." She pointed her finger at the page. "They live in a cocoon. We saw those, too."

"The cocoon is a safe place for the caterpillar until they're ready to fly. But they can't stay there forever."

Sophie frowned. "Why is it a safe place?"

"It protects them from anything that might hurt the caterpillar. Birds think the caterpillar makes a great snack."

Sophie shuddered. "Ugh. I like doughnuts."

Juliet laughed. "Me, too. Cocoons are wonderful places, giving the caterpillar time to grow stronger and braver so they don't become some bird's snack. Your house is kind of like your cocoon."

The child went still. "But it's scary out there, Miss Juliet," she whispered. "I'm afraid."

Her expression broke Juliet's heart.

"I am so sorry what happened to you and your dad that day. Sometimes the world can be a scary place." It was important to validate the child's feelings. "I totally understand why you'd be scared after what happened. I would be, too."

Yet it was also important to move on. Dwelling on the scary thing could be as harmful as not acknowledging it.

She placed her hands on either side of Sophie's face. "But the world isn't always scary. There's a lot of good in it. A lot of beauty. A lot of happiness."

"Like the butterflies?"

"Just like the butterflies." She drew the child into the circle of her arm. "I also think caterpillars might get lonely if they stayed in the cocoon forever. Like you missing your school friends."

Sophie bit her lip. "I hadn't thought about that."

"Think about everything they would miss if they never leave the cocoon. They'd never get to open their new wings."

Sophie held up her index finger. "Or see the flowers."

"Exactly. Or catch the breeze and soar through the sky with their friends. Never do anything fun or become the beautiful creatures God made them to be."

Sophie rested her head under Juliet's chin. "Do you think they're afraid when they come out of the cocoon?"

Juliet swallowed. "I think they probably are, but sometimes we have to choose to be brave so we don't miss out on the wonderful."

The little girl sighed. "I want to be brave like the flutterbies, Miss Juliet. But I don't know how."

"Would you let Moose, your dad and me help you feel braver, Sophie? We'll take it slow, one step at a time, until you can handle the fear without our help."

"I'd like that." She turned her face into Juliet's collar. "You and Moose and Daddy make me feel safe."

At a creak in the floorboards, Juliet looked over Sophie's head to find Rob standing on the threshold.

His Adam's apple bobbed in his throat. "Thank you."

It was the breakthrough they'd been waiting for. She felt drained from the intensity of the emotions. Moose barked and scampered around Rob.

Sophie squatted beside the little dog. "Did you miss me, Moosie-Moose?"

Moose licked her face.

"It's about time for Moose to take a break, Soph." Reaching down, she laid her hand upon the child's silky-smooth hair. "Maybe you could use one, too."

Scowling, Sophie rose. "Naps are for babies." She jutted her chin.

"Uh-oh." He chuckled. "Now you've done it."

She laid her hand on Sophie's shoulder. "You are absolutely not a baby."

He rolled his eyes. "Kids never want to nap. And adults wish they could have one."

Amused, her gaze flitted to him. His hands braced against both sides of the door frame, he grinned.

Her pulse jackhammering, she wrenched her attention to Sophie. "Big kids, however, do have quiet times. Moose has a rest every afternoon. He'd love to cuddle with you on the sofa. Maybe you could show him the pictures in the caterpillar book."

"I can read the story to him, Miss Juliet. I'm a big girl."

"Wow." Juliet hugged her. "What a smart four-year-old you are."

"I can't read all the words, but I can read most of them."

"Let me take off Moose's vest first." Juliet unbuckled the purple harness. "Now he'll know he can relax."

Tucking the book under her arm, Sophie beckoned the dog to the sofa. "Come on, Moosie-Moose. It's story time."

"Almost forgot." Juliet rummaged through the Paw

Pals backpack. "He'll want his favorite cuddle toy." She waved the camel-brown plush toy.

Rob blinked. "Is that a moose?"

Sophie lifted Moose onto the cushions. "What else would Moose play with but another moose?"

Juliet waved the toy. "This is Fluff-Fluff." Spotting his best friend, Moose barked, his whole body wriggling.

Rob shook his head. "That ratty old—"

"Shhh, Daddy. Moose will hear you."

Rob made a face. "He's certainly got big enough ears to—"

"Daddy, stop!" Sophie made an attempt to cover Moose's fluffy ears. "You'll hurt his feelings."

"Moose sees himself as invincible and fierce as, well…" Juliet stuck her tongue in her cheek. "As a moose."

The little dog yipped to remind her he was waiting for Fluff-Fluff.

Juliet extended the much-loved, much-worn stuffed animal to Moose. Growling happily, he seized the toy between his teeth. Sophie settled onto the cushions.

Fluff-Fluff clutched in his mouth, Moose did a tiny three-sixty before curling in the crook of Sophie's arm. They snuggled as she read to Moose.

Juliet watched them for a few seconds to make sure they were settling in nicely. "You've done a beautiful job with her, Rob." She strolled back to the table.

"Not just me." Keeping his voice low, he joined her. "Miss Geraldine has made it her personal mission to come over here several times a week since the…" He shot a look at the couch. "…the incident to make sure she didn't miss out on everything her preschool class was doing."

From the living room, Sophie's voice continued uninterrupted in her reading to Moose.

Juliet smiled. "God bless the Knit-Knackers."

"Pesky as they are, they do have kind hearts. I'm not sure how Soph and I would've coped without them. After Katrina died, I wasn't sure we'd make it. But with God's help and a lot of community support, we're doing well. And thanks to you, I have hope we'll emerge from this latest crisis even stronger."

Juliet sat down at the table. His words about the Laurel Grove community hit too close to home for her liking. She gathered the craft supplies. Maybe that's why she continued to flounder. Her unwillingness to allow anyone to help her.

Over the years the Knit-Knackers had tried to be there for her, but she'd not allowed herself the luxury of community support. Perhaps she had it all wrong. Maybe community wasn't a luxury, but a necessity.

Her mom was right. Time and space weren't proving enough. Not if she wanted to get better. For the first time in five years, she did want to be better.

"Would you mind telling me more about what happened that day at the store?" Juliet lowered her voice. "I feel like I'm missing a few pieces of the puzzle."

He sank into the chair beside her. "After the first shot, there was chaos. But the shooter was standing between the crowd and the exit."

She stopped tidying the table. "I can't imagine how terrifying that must've been."

He shook his head. "That's just the thing. In those situations, my heart starts racing, my blood gets to pumping and my instincts take over. But this time they failed me."

"They didn't fail you. You're a hero."

"Don't say that. It's not true. I should've stayed with Sophie." He tucked in his chin. "I should've never left her. But all I could think to do was hide her. We were in the outdoor patio section."

"I thought you were there to buy a birthday gift for one of Sophie's preschool friends."

"We were, but I was also in the market for a new patio set, and we'd walked over to that department first." He scraped his hand over his face. "I thank God we were there. Or else I might not have been able to find cover for Sophie. When the shots rang out, she was scared." He grimaced. "I was scared."

Juliet edged forward. Her knee brushed against his under the table. "Courage isn't the absence of fear, but the willingness to do the hard thing anyway."

"I hid her in one of those wicker deck bins where you store cushions." He leaned closer, so as not to be overheard in the living room. "She clung to me. Begged me not to leave her. I told her I had to. But did I really have to leave her? I've told myself a thousand times that I did, but I'm not so sure. My line of work tends to attract adrenaline junkies like me. I told her to lay very still and not to move until I came back."

Juliet couldn't imagine how frightened Sophie must have been in the dark storage bin, hearing gunshots and cries of pain.

"I'm glad Sophie didn't see you get shot."

"No, but she saw the blood on my leg when I returned and lifted her out. I can't believe she doesn't hate me. I hate myself for leaving her."

He clenched his fist.

"Sophie doesn't hate you." Juliet laid her hand over his. She couldn't allow him to beat himself up. She had to try to comfort him, to reassure him as she'd reassured his daughter. "Sophie loves you. More than anyone. And the idea of losing you… It's temporarily thrown her for a loop."

"Temporarily? Are you sure?" His voice sounded choked.

"It's going to be okay."

They both cut a glance to the sofa where Sophie was reading another book to Moose, something about a teddy bear.

"Maybe not right this minute, but it's going to be all right, Rob. Often we have to endure the worst before we get to the best."

"But did it have to be me? I left my four-year-old child alone with a gunman on a rampage." He scrubbed his face with his hand. "What's wrong with me? Do I have some kind of rescuer complex that drove me to intervene?"

"There's absolutely nothing wrong with you. As a police officer, you have skills no one else in that store had. If you hadn't stopped the shooter, more people would've been hurt. It's a blessing that no one died."

"This may sound cold, but honestly none of it would've been worth it if it had cost me Sophie." He grimaced. "I'm not only a terrible father, but a terrible person, too."

She squeezed his hand. "You are too hard on yourself. I can't comprehend the kind of pressure you were under in that moment. There were no perfect options. You had to make a split-second decision."

He took a ragged breath. "I made the wrong choice. For my child."

"The gunman was systematically going from department to department. And you ran toward him. Don't you see? In saving the others, you saved her, too."

He lifted his head. "You really think so?" he rasped.

"I do."

"Thank you."

She stared at him. "For what?"

"For letting me think out loud. I haven't told anyone about how torn up I've been by the guilt."

"Misplaced guilt. You did what you had to do. You saved everyone's life in the process, including the shooter's by stopping him. Like I told you before, guilt isn't a productive use of time."

"You're easy to talk to."

She was glad he thought so. He and Sophie were both so easy to be with. Too easy.

At almost the same instant, they each became aware of how quiet Sophie had become. He started to rise.

"Let me." Tiptoeing over, Juliet peered over the sofa. "Sophie and Moose are asleep," she whispered. "And she has her arm around him." Juliet returned to the table.

"Earlier you said something that made me think… Have you struggled with guilt, too? About your husband's death?"

She stiffened. Why had she let that slip? To him of all people?

Yet time after time, he somehow managed to slip past her defenses. Circumventing the wall she'd erected around her pain and confusion.

Was it time to finally admit she couldn't get through her grief on her own? Could she be as brave as Sophie? Could she allow him to see her pain? Yet where did she begin? But she knew. Same as what she'd said to Sophie.

One small, slow step at a time.

He'd trusted her with his deepest internal conflicts. It wasn't something she regarded lightly. If she was a true friend, shouldn't she do the same?

"My *guilt* has nothing to do with Josh's death." She lifted her gaze to meet his. "My guilt is wrapped up in losing his child."

* * *

Rob went still. The pain in her dark eyes took his breath.

"I was four months pregnant when Josh…" She sucked in a breath. "When Josh was killed in combat. Two days later, I miscarried our son."

Abruptly, she dropped her gaze. She raised her hands to the table. Then she lowered them to her lap.

"I'm sorry, Juliet. I didn't realize you'd lost a child. I don't know how I would've survived Katrina's death without Sophie. You must've been devastated."

Avoiding his eyes, she picked up the scissors and a roll of tape. "I blame myself entirely. If only we hadn't waited to have a baby."

Juliet cut strip after strip. Perhaps it was easier for her to tell the story if her hands were busy.

"I was working on my counseling degree, and Josh was concentrating on his military career. If only I'd coped with the news of his death better. If only I'd taken better care of myself, but losing him was such a shock."

"The if-onlys are eating you alive, Juliet."

She looked at him then. "You're right," she whispered.

For a long moment, their gazes locked. And in that moment, she allowed him a tiny glimpse of her heart. The sadness in those beautiful brown eyes shook him to his core.

An unfamiliar desire to protect her surged in his chest. Like a raindrop on a pane of glass, a single tear made a sliding trek down her cheek. He caught the tear with his finger.

Rob held out the teardrop. "Kiss away the sorrow for the brightness of tomorrow."

Her brow furrowed. "Is that a nursery rhyme?"

"Think of it as a grown-up version of kissing away a boo-boo."

She narrowed her eyes at him. "You made it up."

He grinned. "So what if I did? Go ahead," he urged. "What can it hurt?"

The corners of her mouth curved. "You want me to actually kiss my own tear? On your finger?"

"I dare you." His stomach knotted. "I can't stand to see you cry, Juliet."

Blinking rapidly, she opened her mouth as if to speak and then closed it.

Great. The idea of kissing even his finger rendered her speechless with disbelief.

I'm an idiot.

What had he been thinking? He hadn't been thinking. Or maybe the truth was, he'd found the courage to finally say exactly what he'd been thinking.

He'd wanted to kiss her since the first moment they met. He prepared himself for her to flee. She would probably drop their case, return to Greensboro, and Sophie would be the one—yet again—to bear the brunt of his ill-advised madness.

"Did you say you *dare* me, Rob Melbourne?" An interesting glint entered her expressive eyes.

Not sure what he'd unleashed, his heartbeat accelerated a notch. "I… I did."

She pursed her lips. "You don't believe I'll do it, do you?"

"I… I…"

Resting her arms on the table, she leaned forward. In their attempt to keep their conversation hushed, their foreheads were almost touching.

She eyed the teardrop on his finger. "Kiss away the sorrow, huh?"

He nodded. "For the brightness of tomorrow."

She inhaled softly. "Okay then, here's to tomorrow."

She brushed her lips in a featherlight kiss across his finger. His heart dropped in his chest.

Juliet sat back.

His finger tingled, still feeling the warmth of her breath. "Kissing away the sadness."

"Bringing in the gladness?"

He nodded.

Flushing a becoming shade of pink, her eyes found his. "I hope so."

So did he. There passed between them something inexplicable. Something new. And altogether wonderful.

"Daddy?" Sophie's head popped up over the back of the sofa.

They jerked apart. Not to be outdone, Moose barked from the other side of the cushions.

Recovering first, Juliet jumped up from the table. "Did you and Moose have a nice rest? I want to teach you some breathing exercises for you to practice the next time you feel anxious."

For the next thirty minutes, she became brisk, the consummate professional, and impersonal, at least toward him.

"Breathe in slowly while I count to three. Good girl. Now breathe out a big, deep belly breath while I count again to three." She smiled at his daughter. "Excellent."

They ran through the exercise several times with Sophie taking turns blowing a feather to the count of three.

"You were such a brave girl to do exactly what Daddy told you to do that day at the store." Juliet hugged her. "Lie on your back this time, please."

Juliet placed the tiny dog on her chest. Moose licked her chin. Sophie chuckled.

"Why don't you practice by blowing on Moose's fluffy fur?"

"Moose helping me feel brave is fun." Sophie's belly rumbled with laughter. "Thank you, Miss Juliet."

Juliet's mouth quivered. "You're very very welcome, Sophie."

She returned to the table. One day, she would make some child a wonderful mother. He hadn't realized he'd said that out loud until her smile fell away.

Her eyes darkened. "I won't ever be anyone's mother."

"I'm sorry. I didn't realize because of the miscarriage you couldn't—"

"*Won't* doesn't mean *can't*," she snapped.

His gaze darted to Sophie, but she and Moose had gone over to the toy corner.

"I meant— One day, you'll marry again."

She gave him a blistering look. "I will *not* marry again. I adore children, but there won't be a child in my life other than the ones I meet through my work with Paw Pals."

"But why?" He opened his hands. "You could foster. You could—"

"They wouldn't be Josh's child."

"That is the most…" He gritted his teeth. "You're telling me you would close your heart to someone like me, who lost both parents, because you're punishing yourself for losing your baby? For something completely beyond your control?"

"That's not…" Confusion clouded her eyes. "Grief— my kind of grief—is a complicated thing."

"Apparently. Thank God in my time of need, Aunt Evie and Uncle Adrian didn't feel the same as you." He pushed back his chair. "I think we've done about all we can do here for today, don't you?"

Juliet rose. "On that we agree."

She called for Moose, said her goodbyes to Sophie and left.

Watching her drive away, he felt sick inside. He told himself he ought to be glad he knew where she stood on a wide range of issues that were important to him.

Like family. And faith. Before he or Sophie got any deeper into a relationship with her.

He raked his hand over his head. He'd had a narrow escape indeed. Good that he'd wised up.

Now if only he could convince his heart.

Chapter Seven

Driving to her mom's house, Juliet fretted over her heated words with Rob.

Why had she said those things to him? Was he right? Was her refusal to open her heart because she was still punishing herself for losing Josh's baby?

He was your baby, too.

If that was truly what she was doing, it wasn't only wrongheaded but unhealthy.

Troubled, she went into the house and fed Moose. He needed to let off some energy so she put him in the backyard to play.

Smiling, she watched him explore for a few minutes. Then turning away from the expansive yard of the old house, she checked the calendar on the inside of the pantry door.

There was a notation in the square for Wednesday. *Dr. Woodbridge, 10 a.m.*

She updated Sophie's electronic file and talked with Mrs. Larsen at the hospital, who was overseeing Sophie's case, regarding today's progress. Still waiting for her mom to get off work, she put together a simple dinner for them.

The gingerbread Queen Victorian had been in her family for four generations. The first Mitchell arrived in Laurel Grove at the turn of the twentieth century to become the manager at one of the textile mills for which the area was still renowned. The house had been her grandfather's pride and joy. Over the years, he and her mother lovingly restored the house to its original condition.

Juliet had grown up with many happy memories in this house. Now her grandfather was gone. But she would make sure her mom understood she was here for her.

She brought their plates to the table on the wraparound porch just as her mother's green Subaru pulled into the driveway.

Knitting tote on her shoulder, stuffed with business orders and of course, yarn, her mom came up the steps. "What a lovely surprise. Where's Moose?"

"He's enjoying doggie time in the backyard. It's such a wonderful evening. Not too humid yet. I thought it would be nice to eat outside for a change."

Setting the tote on the gray planked floor, her mother sat down. "Sharing a meal with my favorite person is always a treat. Anytime. Anywhere."

With the scent of magnolia wafting over them, they ate in silence for a few moments.

Then Juliet cleared her throat. "Are you interested in how the day went with Sophie?"

"I didn't want to pry." Her mom waved her fork. "Client confidentiality and all that."

Juliet blew out a breath. "Forgive me for being so touchy yesterday. This case had me more nervous than I realized."

"The case or the people?"

"Both." She sipped from her iced tea. "It's tricky when you're friends with the client. Sophie and I have established a good rapport. I've never seen Moose take to a child like he has Sophie. I'm optimistic about her progress."

Her mother raised a slim eyebrow. "Is that what you are? Friends with Rob Melbourne?"

After their disagreement, she hoped he was still her friend. The idea of losing his respect gutted her in a way she hadn't expected. Why had she lashed out at him?

She pleated the napkin in her lap. "It would be unprofessional for me to be anything more than a friend."

"Until Sophie is no longer under your care."

"Mom… Don't start on that again."

"Okay. Okay." Her mother held up her hand. "I won't push, but I remember how much you always liked him. You'd get tongue-tied whenever you ran into him at the farm."

Had she really been that obvious? A wave of heat washed up her neck. She felt sure Rob had been too busy with sports and his active social life to notice. Or at least, that's what she fervently hoped.

She took a sip of tea. "Rob has that effect on females of every age. Not just me."

Her mom frowned. "I never pictured Rob as a player."

Bursting out laughing, she set her glass down before she spilled it. "Look at you, Mom. Keeping up with the lingo. Rob has never been a player. Charm just oozes from him. He can't help it."

"I do my best to stay current." Her mother tossed Juliet an impudent grin. "And culturally relevant."

"You are very relevant to me, Mom. And I'm sorry if I failed to communicate that clearly to you over the last five years."

Perhaps this was the opening she'd been searching for.

"There's a note on the calendar for tomorrow. Who is Dr. Woodbridge, and why are you going to see him?"

"You saw that?" Her mother slumped. "Dr. Woodbridge is a she."

"What's going on, Mom?" She leaned forward. "Please don't shut me out."

Her mother gave her a sharp look.

She sighed. "I'm sorry for shutting you out for so long from my pain. It was all I could do to take the next breath. I didn't want to bring anyone else into my misery."

Her mom reached across the table for her hand. "A mother is only as happy as her saddest child. Your pain is my pain. For a parent, there's no way around it. Whether you choose to share it with me or not."

Juliet recalled Rob's anguish over Sophie. "I'm beginning to understand that. Coming home…" She scanned the oak-lined street. "It's reminded me we all need someone to help us through the sorrow. Please tell me what's going on." She squeezed her mother's hand.

Her mom gave a shaky laugh. "I've had three abnormal Pap tests."

She sucked in a breath. "What does that mean? Does the doctor think you have cancer?"

"Dr. Woodbridge is not using that word…yet. Test results are sometimes inconclusive. She said most women who have abnormal results don't have cervical cancer."

"So what's the next step?"

Her mother straightened. "She wants to do a colposcopy and take a biopsy of the cell tissue in her office tomorrow at the women's center in Greensboro."

She got out of her chair and came around the table. "I'm going with you." She put her arm around her mother.

"I appreciate your offer, darling, but you have your

work with Moose and Sophie. Evelyn will drive me. I won't be alone."

She crouched beside her mom's chair. "Nothing is more important than your health. I can drive you just as well as Evelyn. I want to be there." Her voice thickened. "Please. I need to be there with you."

Her mother's dark eyes probed Juliet's features. Whatever she saw there apparently satisfied her. "All right. But what about your work with Sophie? I hate for her to lose momentum."

"If I take you to the doctor, maybe Evelyn could stay with you in the afternoon and I could spend a few hours with Sophie."

Her mom made a face. "I don't need a babysitter."

"You don't know how you're going to feel. Why not enjoy your best friend's company until I return?"

"If you're sure this isn't going to be a problem for Sophie…"

Resuming her seat, Juliet fluttered her hand. "I'm sure. I'll text Rob right now." Actually, after the way things had ended between them earlier, she wasn't sure. But just as Sophie came first with Rob, Juliet's mother had to come first with her.

Pulling out her phone, she started texting, then looked up. "Is it all right for Rob to know what's going on with you?"

"I have no problem with him knowing." Her mom arched her brows. "Since Rob is not my client, just my friend."

She rolled her eyes.

Her mother's lips twitched. "I'd appreciate his prayers."

She sent a quick text explaining the situation and asked if they could meet in the afternoon. Stomach churning, she hit Send. Putting her phone beside her plate, she took a few bites before her cell dinged.

Reading the incoming message, the tightness in her chest eased. He readily agreed to the change in plans and sent his well-wishes to her mom.

She thanked him, put down the phone and resumed eating. Her cell lit up again. Another text from Rob. Would you consider leaving Moose with us for the day?

Usually, she took Moose everywhere with her. But waiting in a doctor's office during her mom's procedure was not going to work. Her policy at Paw Pals was for the dog handler to always be present with the canine and patients.

However, if he wasn't working... If he was just being Moose... Sophie loved him so much. And Moose loved her right back.

She typed. Butterfly ears growing on you? M & I accept. Drop him off at 9? Btw I'm sorry for earlier.

Almost immediately, there was a response. Butterfly ears not the only thing growing on me. See u then. I'm sorry, too.

He ended with a smiley emoji. Which prompted a smile of her own.

"You seem pleased about something."

She put her phone away. "Moose is having a just-for-fun playdate with Sophie tomorrow while we're gone."

"Just-for-fun playdates are essential for humans, too. Maybe you and Rob should plan one."

"Mother!" she moaned.

"Glad to see you haven't lost your sense of humor. A month ago, you would've bit my head off for making such a suggestion. Or worse, burst into tears."

Her mom wasn't wrong. Even three days ago, Juliet might've reacted like that.

"You do seem better. Better than I've seen you in a long time. More relaxed. Dare I say, even happier?"

"Happier might be a stretch." But more at peace? Juliet would give her that.

"I wonder what's made the difference." Her mother gave her a coy look. "I'd love to take the credit but…"

"You and Laurel Grove have definitely made a difference. The slower pace." Juliet motioned at the table. "Dinner on the porch. Seeing old friends."

As soon as she said it, she realized her mistake. A mistake her mom pounced upon with no small amount of glee.

"Old friends like Rob Melbourne?"

Juliet gave her a look. "You're not going to let that go, are you?"

Her mother's mouth curved. "Not on your life, darling."

A change of topic was overdue.

"Mom, could you help me with a small craft project? I've had an idea for something to help Sophie."

She explained about the breathing exercises she'd taught Sophie to self-regulate her emotions when the little girl felt anxious. And also how amazingly the child had fallen asleep with Moose by her side.

Her mother nodded. "She's had a terrible time sleeping since the shooting. Moose made her feel secure enough to drift off to sleep."

"So I thought why not give her the Moose Effect every night?" Juliet perched on the edge of her seat. "Would you help me create a small stuffed toy replica of Moose out of yarn?"

Her mom propped her elbows on the table. "Felted wool might work."

She could practically see the wheels turning in her mother's brain.

"Crochet would probably be better."

Juliet sagged. "Is that going to be a problem? You're a knitter."

Her mom winked. "No, my craft-challenged daughter. I happen to be multitalented."

"Not a surprise to me. You're an inspiration." She locked eyes with her mother. "I'm so proud of how you raised me on your own and how you've become such a successful businesswoman."

As usual, her mom shrugged off any hint of praise. "I did what I had to do to take care of you. I'm very blessed that by exploring a particular passion, I was also able to return home to Laurel Grove and make a living."

"I wish I was more like you."

"You're doing valuable work with Paw Pals, your personal passion. I've no doubt when the hospital board reviews how you've helped Sophie, you'll be a shoo-in for the start-up grant."

"I hope so. Although, I've gotten so involved with Sophie I haven't thought much about the grant."

After dinner, her mother worked out a design with Juliet and searched through her personal yarn inventory to find the right colors for the tricolor Moose.

"You don't have to start on this tonight, Mom."

Her mother rummaged through her yarn organizer for a particular taffy shade. "I need to keep my hands busy so I don't think about tomorrow."

Juliet picked up a skein of soft, white yarn. "Try not to worry. We're in this together."

The next morning, she left her mom in the car and brought Moose to the Melbournes's front door. Waiting for Rob to answer her knock, her chest tightened.

Would he still be angry with her? Had she ruined the easy camaraderie between them?

Rob opened the door. His bare feet poked out from his jeans. Her stomach did a crazy flip-flop.

When not with him, somehow she always forgot how ruggedly appealing he truly was. Until she was face-to-face with him again.

The better she got to know him—and see him interact with Sophie—the more she realized his appeal was more about his character and less to do with his looks.

He ran his hand over his hair, still damp from the shower. "Mornin', Jules." Eyes crinkling, he stuck his hands in his pockets.

Butterflies fluttered in her belly. "Good morning."

Any morning involving Rob Melbourne was sure to be a great morning.

Sophie ran forward. "Hi, Miss Juliet. Hi, Moose."

The little dog barked.

"I'll take real good care of Moose while you're with your mommy, Miss Juliet. I promise."

Juliet handed the leash to her. "I know you will." She took the backpack off her shoulder. "I've also brought some of Moose's toys."

Sophie perked. "Fluff-Fluff? Moose might want to take a rest."

"Water. Food bowl." Juliet patted the backpack. "And yes, Fluff-Fluff, too." She looked at Rob. "Another rough night?"

Nodding, he rubbed the back of his neck.

"I'm working on an idea to help. And Rob?" She moistened her lips. "I'm sorry for yesterday. I didn't like the way we left things. Are we okay?"

"I didn't like the way we left things, either. I had no right to tell you how to feel." He gave her a crooked smile, setting off the topsy-turvy feeling in her belly again, leaving her feeling oddly breathless. "And yes, we're okay."

Taking the backpack, Sophie led Moose over to the couch. Moose seemed content with Sophie. He would be fine.

But it felt strange leaving her furry companion behind. Over the last three years, she'd spent far more time in his canine company than with humans. If she'd had a child, this was similar to what she imagined she might feel after dropping them off for their first day of kindergarten. It was kind of gut-wrenching. More than a little bittersweet.

However, there was no time for protracted farewells.

"Bye, Sophie. Bye, Moose," she called. "See you this afternoon."

Sophie ran over and gave her a big hug. "Moose and I will pray for your mommy."

Juliet hugged her back, taking a moment to breathe in the sweet, little girl scent of her. "Thank you, darling."

The child pulled away. "I can't wait to show Moosie-Moose my toys." She headed toward the hall.

Hearing his name, Moose trotted over, barked and licked Juliet's ankle before scooting after Sophie.

Juliet gazed after them for a second. There was no question she needed Moose far more than the tiny dog needed her.

Rob leaned his shoulder against the door frame. "I hope the procedure goes well for your mother."

She took a breath. "Thank you."

"I'll work with Sophie this morning to create some goals for the rest of the week."

"That would be wonderful." She smiled. "I can't guarantee what time I'll return this afternoon. You never know how long it will take at the doctor's office."

"Don't worry about us." He held the door for her. "Take care of your mom. We'll see you later."

When she slid behind the wheel of her car, Juliet's mother set aside the crochet hook and yarn she'd been working on. "Everything okay?"

She nodded and put the key in the ignition. "Ready?"

Her mom sighed. "As ready as I'll ever be."

Juliet cast one final glance at the house. As ready as she'd ever be, too. But she wasn't thinking about a surgical procedure.

She was thinking about the state of her heart.

While Sophie tried teaching Moose some new tricks, Rob fielded a phone call from his chief in Greensboro. The guys at the station had been great about checking on him while he was on leave.

He clicked off and scrubbed his forehead. He got why Juliet had thrown herself so completely into building Paw Pals.

Transferring to the Greensboro PD, he'd done the same. Pouring himself into each case. Out to prove his worth to a new boss. And fill the empty hours without Katrina.

But the long hours of the job, especially the first seventy-two hours at the beginning of a case, weren't sustainable in the long run for a single dad like himself. It wasn't fair to Sophie. And it was becoming increasingly clear to him that her well-being was the only thing that truly mattered.

He was contemplating a career change. Although, he hadn't shared his plans with anyone yet. There was the whole issue of finding another decent-paying job. Laurel Grove wasn't exactly a hotbed of opportunity. Most folks made the commute to Greensboro every day.

"Daddy." Kneeling beside the fluffy canine, Sophie waved him over. "Moose wants to shake hands."

"Is that right?" Rob eased off the sofa to the carpet, and wondered just how painful it was going to be to get back to his feet. "Show me what you got, little dude."

"Shake, Moose." Sophie clasped her hands under her chin. "Shake Daddy's hand."

On his haunches, Moose lifted one tiny paw. Rob gave it a gentle shake.

"Good boy!" Sophie fished a small treat from the backpack. Moose snatched it up. "Isn't he a good boy, Daddy?" She flashed him a smile. "The best dog ever."

"The best." He tugged her into a hug. "And you're the best little girl." Thinking about what could have happened to her that day made him physically ill.

Sophie pulled away, eager to show him what else she'd taught Moose. "Gimme five, Moosie-Moose."

Moose slapped his paw into her upraised palm. She giggled.

"Soph?"

His daughter gave Moose another small treat. Moose licked his jowls. "Yes, Daddy?"

"Can we talk for a minute?"

Hearing the seriousness of his voice, she sidled closer to him. "What is it, Daddy?"

Leaning against the skirt of the sofa, he tucked her underneath his arm. "I don't think I've ever told you how sorry I am for leaving you alone in the bin at the store. I shouldn't have done that. I'm…" His heart pinched. "I'm so, so sorry. But I promise you, honey, I'm going to get a different job so I can be with you more."

She tilted up her heart-shaped face. "Does that mean you won't be a policeman anymore?"

He swallowed. "Yes."

"Do you like being a policeman, Daddy?"

He took a breath. "Yes, but—"

"You're good at being a policeman." A crease marred the smooth bridge of her small nose. "I heard you and Miss Juliet talking yesterday. She said you saved a lot of people."

"I'll always regret leaving you, Soph." His eyes stung. "You were so afraid."

God forgive him, she still is.

"I was scared." She worried her lower lip with her baby teeth. "But Miss Juliet is helping me feel brave again. She said you're brave."

He shook his head. "I just did what a policeman should do."

"Did those people have little girls and little boys and little dogs waiting for them at their homes?"

He looked into her serene gaze. "Probably some did."

"Then see." She cradled his face between the warm, small palms of her hands. "You did the helping thing you were supposed to do. Like God made Moose to help me. Don't feel sad, my daddy. It's okay."

Sophie hadn't called him "my daddy" since she was a toddler. Since her mother died. And for the first time since the sound of gunfire rang out in the big-box store, he believed they might actually be okay.

"I love you, Sophie girl."

She hugged him. "I love you, Daddy."

Moose barked.

She grinned. "I love you, too, Moosie-Moose." Reaching for him, she pulled him into their hugfest.

After a while, she let go of Rob. She kept one arm, however, slung around Moose's neck. "I feel like doing something brave today, Daddy."

"You…you do?" He tried to steady the tremble in his voice. "What would you like to do?"

Finger on her chin, she surveyed the room. "I think I would like to have a tea party on the porch with Moose."

"That sounds like a great idea. The back porch?"

She shook her head. "Nope. The front porch."

"Wow." He put his hand on her head. "That's so brave of you to start there."

Sophie's eyes lit with pride. "Miss Juliet says I'm a very brave girl."

His heart swelled for love of this precious child of his.

"I don't want to miss the good stuff Miss Juliet and I talked about. So we need to make a plan so I can get braver every day."

"Let's do it."

Jumping up, she ran to the kitchen junk drawer and removed several objects. She thrust a pad of paper and a pencil at him. "I'll tell you what to write."

He grinned. "Why, yes, Soph. I'd be happy to be your administrative assistant. What are you thinking?"

They spent the next fifteen minutes outlining an ever-widening circle for her to master. The porch, followed by a drive in the car to the farm to show Aunt Evie and Uncle Adrian how brave she was.

"Then we should visit Miss Juliet's mom to tell her we hope she feels better soon."

He jotted a note. "That's a good idea."

"But Miss Lesley is usually at her store."

He paused writing. "It's a nice place. She has a box of toys there for little kids when they visit."

Sophie's lower lip wobbled. "I don't know if I feel brave enough to go into a store, Daddy."

"If you don't feel ready yet, I'm sure Miss Lesley would come out to the car and say hello."

She touched the tip of her finger to the end of the page. "Maybe just put 'Go into Miss Lesley's store' at the bottom of the list, Daddy."

"Got it."

"And we should get ice cream with Miss Juliet."

Bending over the paper, he hid a smile. "The drive-through?"

"If Miss Juliet holds my hand, I think I'll be brave enough to go inside for ice cream."

He added the item with a flourish.

As for the difference between the knit shop and the ice cream shop? Sophie was definitely her father's daughter. There weren't many things that would keep him away from an ice cream cone, either.

"One more thing, Daddy."

"What's that?"

"I want to take Moose to my class at school to show his tricks."

He scratched his cheek with the tip of the eraser. "School is letting out for the summer in a few weeks, Soph."

Would Sophie feel up to returning to school that soon? Juliet and Moose might not be around, either. A thought that filled him with no small amount of dread.

"We'll have to make me brave fast, Daddy."

He didn't want to raise her hopes only to have them crushed. "We'll have to ask Miss Juliet if it's okay for Moose to go to school."

Sophie clapped her hands. "Everybody will laugh so hard to see a moose at school. Aren't I silly?"

"The silliest."

She bounced up. "Let's make cookies for the tea party."

Catching her excitement, Moose ran rings around the coffee table, barking.

Rob shifted and bit back a groan. "First, though?" Thankful for his strong, resilient daughter, he held out his hand. "You're going to have to help your poor old dad get off the floor."

Chapter Eight

The morning flew by for Rob. He and Sophie spent the next hour baking cookies.

Seeing the recipe written out by Katrina brought a wave of momentary sadness. He quickly countered, as he'd learned to do, with an accompanying wave of gratitude.

One day, Sophie would be thrilled to have this sample of her mother's handwriting. And how happy it would've made Katrina to know they were making her cinnamon–chocolate chip cookies.

After lunch, he moved the small plastic table and chairs from Sophie's bedroom to the front porch. Back in the kitchen, he placed the child-sized plastic cups and saucers on a serving tray. Tail swishing like a fluffy windshield wiper, Moose followed him to the front door.

Carrying the plate of cookies, Sophie touched his arm. "Let me go first, Daddy." Moose barked.

He smiled. "Okay." He waited. His smile fell. "Sophie?"

She stared beyond the open door to the street. Cars drove past their house. Neighbors, including Miss Geraldine's husband, worked in their yards. The aroma of fresh-mown grass filled his nostrils.

A squirrel chittered. A slight breeze lifted tiny tendrils of hair around her ears. But lips thin, she didn't move. With a sympathetic whine, Moose rubbed his face against her leg.

Juliet was right about the small dog. He always appeared to know when someone needed his encouragement.

"We don't have to do this today, Soph."

The fear on her face felt like a knife plunged in his heart. In her desire to please him, had he pushed her into something she wasn't ready for? Desperately, he tried to recall everything Juliet had advised. Striking the balance between support and doing too much was tricky.

He angled toward the living room. "We can try this another time."

Barking, Moose nudged her leg.

She took a huge breath and exhaled slowly. Practicing the breathing exercise Juliet had taught her to do when anxiety overwhelmed her.

"I'm ready, Daddy." Taking a step forward, she glanced over her shoulder at him. "Watch me."

His throat tightened. "I'm watching, honey," he rasped.

She stepped onto the porch. Moose bounded over the threshold right behind her.

Whirling, she gazed back at Rob. "I did it, Daddy." Her blue eyes shone. "I did it."

Moose pranced around her, his tail whipping like a metronome.

Rob's eyes misted. "I'm so proud of you, Sophie."

"Come on, Daddy," she beckoned. "What're you waiting for?"

He joined her and Moose on the porch.

Suddenly becoming brisk, she took charge of unloading the tray and setting the tea table. Funny enough, that brought Juliet to his mind.

He deposited Moose on top of a pile of dictionaries in one of the chairs.

She motioned him to another chair. "You sit here, Daddy."

He crammed his large frame into the child-sized chair. And while some men might find it beneath their dignity to be seen having a tea party on the front porch for all to see, he'd do just about anything to keep the smile on his little girl's face.

With a flourish, she poured lemonade from the plastic teapot into the plastic cups. Pink lemonade, of course. Moose watched the entire proceedings with a dignified calm. As if tea parties were an everyday occurrence for him.

For all Rob knew, perhaps they were.

Posture erect, ankles crossed, she held out the plate of cookies. "Would you care for a cookie, Mr. Melbourne?"

She reminded him of Miss Helen, the prim and proper old pastor's wife. He could totally envision tea parties being Miss Helen's sort of thing. The Knit-Knackers had taken his daughter into their hearts as if she were one of their own grandchildren.

He reached for a cookie, or two. "Why thank you, Miss Melbourne. Don't mind if I do."

She held out one of Moose's special cookies to him, which he gobbled up. "Doesn't he have wonderful manners? He waited for his turn so patiently."

Definitely echoes of Miss Helen.

"An example we should aspire to follow." Rob lifted his cup. "Is it pinkie in or pinkie out, Miss Melbourne?"

"Pinkie out, Daddy." She arched a look at him over the rim of her cup. "Don't be silly."

Taking a tiny sip, he hid his grin. But give him tea parties any day. Too soon, an idiot boy would want to take her to prom. At the prospect of raising her alone during the teen years, his courage failed him.

And the only woman he'd found attractive since Katrina died had made her thoughts on marriage all too clear.

Yet Uncle Adrian always said, it was a bad wind that never altered. Hearts and minds could be changed. Rob was realizing that he was up for the challenge.

Sophie smiled. "Won't Miss Juliet be surprised to see my tea party?"

Rallying, he returned her smile. "She definitely will."

He couldn't wait to see the expression on her face when she saw Sophie outside. The wait wasn't long. Ten minutes later, she pulled into the driveway.

Moose spotted her first. Leaping from the small chair, he scooted down the steps, barking his enthusiastic greeting.

"Hi, Miss Juliet!" Sophie waved. "Look at me! I'm on the porch! Look at me!"

Breaking into a smile, Juliet scooped Moose into her arms. "I'm so proud of you."

His daughter scuttled around the table. Juliet knelt down to give her a hug.

"Moose missed you, Miss Juliet. I missed you. Daddy missed you." Sophie threw out her arms. "Look how busy we've been."

"I can see that." The funniest look crossed Juliet's face. "Your dad missed me, did he?"

"He did." Rob had been raised to stand in the presence of a lady, but this time, the chair rose with him.

Sophie giggled into her hands. "Daddy looks like a turtle with a shell on his back."

He could tell Juliet was doing her best not to laugh. "Suddenly I've developed a real sympathy for the hunchback of Notre Dame."

Juliet chuckled at his pronunciation. "No-ter Dame is the name of the football school."

"I know that." He folded his arms across his chest, aiming for a cool, hip vibe nearly impossible with a crayon red, child-sized chair attached to him. "Just wanted to make sure you were listening."

This time, she did laugh, pleasing him to no end. He liked making her laugh. He had a feeling she didn't laugh enough. And he was just the man for the job.

She handed Moose into Sophie's open arms and rose. Setting Moose on the gray planked porch, Sophie skipped over to the tea table.

He leaned against one of the porch posts. "You look tired."

Juliet made a wry face. "You really know how to boost a girl's ego." She smothered a smile with her hand. "You look ridiculous."

He grinned. "Thanks."

"You're welcome." She surveyed their tea party. "You two have been busy. You made cookies, too?"

They smiled at each other. And he distinctly felt his heart turn over.

"Daddy and I came up with a plan for the week. The tea party on the porch was first on my Being Brave list."

Juliet exchanged a glance with him. "I can't wait to hear the rest of the list."

Sophie pulled out the green plastic chair next to her. "Have some pink tea with me, Miss Juliet."

"I'd love that. But maybe we should take care of your father first." She cocked her head. "Are you going to be able to get out of that chair?"

"No, I don't think so." He made a show of sighing. "Seems my life has turned into one miniature thing after the other." He smirked. "Including the therapy dog."

Moose barked. Juliet's lips twitched. She extended her hand.

"Better not." He shook his head. "I'm a lot bigger than you. I might sweep you off your feet."

"Is that a warning?" She fluttered her lashes. "I'm stronger than I look."

"Not a warning." He looked at her. "A promise."

She gave an unladylike snort. "What makes you think your charms will work on me?"

He arched his eyebrow. "I'm charming?"

She rolled her eyes. "You'd have to have lived under a rock your entire life not to know the answer to that, Mr. All-State Running Back, Homecoming King, captain of the football team. But consider me immune."

He scowled.

From an early age, he'd been aware that for some reason his smiles got him an extra cookie. Or more time at the playground. That females found his looks to be attractive.

It hadn't meant much to him as a boy. More often than not, he found the attention annoying. He'd been focused on sports, not girls.

He'd spent his teen years hanging out with the crowd versus one specific girl. Of course, that had changed when he'd met Katrina at college.

Aunt Evie and the Knit-Knackers had expended considerable effort in the last year, introducing him to every available woman they knew in the small-town hamlet. None of them intrigued him in the least.

How ironic the only other woman he actually cared about was possibly the one woman in Laurel Grove who didn't find him attractive?

Gritting his teeth, arms gripping the armrests, he struggled to free himself. "I don't… Need your—"

She propped her hands on her slim hips. "Stop being an idiot and let me help you."

"Fine," he grumbled. "Have it your way."

"Always so gracious in defeat."

Despite himself, he laughed.

"Hold on to the post," she directed. "I'm going to free you from your predicament."

He took hold of the pillar.

"On the count of three—"

Sophie jumped up. "Let me count. I know how to count."

Juliet gripped two of the chair legs. "Go ahead, honey."

"One—two—three!"

Juliet yanked with all her might and the chair came away in her hands.

"Yay! You're free, Daddy!" Sophie cheered.

"Thank you." Rob took a step and winced. "Didn't think I was ever getting out of there."

Juliet eyed him. "How's your leg?"

He stiffened. "Good."

"Why don't I believe you? Have you done any stretching exercises today?"

"Like you said," he huffed. "We've been busy."

"Moose could probably use a little exercise. While I have tea with Soph, how about throwing a ball to Moose in the yard? He loves a good game of fetch."

Rob scratched his head. "As a former running back, I'm not unfamiliar with the concept but—"

"While you and Moose play, Sophie can fill me in on the list. Ever-widening circle, remember?"

"Ah." He nodded. "Gotcha."

Spotting Miss Geraldine's husband over the fence weeding the flower bed in his yard, Juliet waved before she turned to Rob. "Moose has a favorite football in the backpack."

"Now you're speaking my language." He picked up Moose. "Us guys got to stick together. Let's have some fun, little dude."

While Rob threw the neon yellow ball and Moose brought it back to him, Sophie told Juliet about her goals, which Juliet noted with no small measure of humor included ice cream. She was also touched to learn of Sophie's concern for Juliet's mom. Such a sweet, caring child.

Somehow during the telling, Sophie slipped onto her lap. It felt like the most natural thing in the world. As if her arms had been made for this child. Which was crazy.

Wasn't it?

The little girl leaned her head against Juliet. "At first, I was scared about going out on the porch, but I breathed like you said."

"You're the bravest girl I know." Juliet hugged her tightly. "Facing the fear the first time is always the hardest. But I promise it gets easier."

If only she could take her own advice…

Venturing out of the house was a huge victory for Sophie. And by mastering her anxiety once, a tremendous boost of confidence for Sophie to tackle the next goal.

"Look at Moose." Sitting forward, Sophie pointed. "When he runs back to Daddy, his ears flutter. Isn't that funny?"

"Very funny," she agreed.

"I want to play ball with Moose." Twisting around, Sophie peered into Juliet's eyes. "Would it be okay if I threw the ball to him?"

Juliet did a silent cheer. Outwardly, she maintained her composure so as not to make a bigger deal of this

Get ready to relax and indulge with your **FREE BOOKS** and more!

Claim up to FOUR NEW BOOKS & TWO MYSTERY GIFTS – absolutely FREE!

Dear Reader,

We both know life can be difficult at times. That's why it's important to treat yourself so you can relax and recharge once in a while.

And I'd like to help you do this by sending you this amazing offer of up to FOUR brand new full length FREE BOOKS that WE pay for.

This is everything I have ready to send to you right now:

Try **Love Inspired® Romance Larger-Print** books and fall in love with inspirational romances that take you on an uplifting journey of faith, forgiveness and hope.

Try **Love Inspired® Suspense Larger-Print** books where courage and optimism unite in stories of faith and love in the face of danger.

Or **TRY BOTH!**

All we ask in return is that you answer 4 simple questions on the attached Treat Yourself survey. You'll get **Two Free Books** and **Two Mystery Gifts** from each series you try, *altogether worth over $20*! Who could pass up a deal like that?

Sincerely,

Pam Powers

Harlequin Reader Service

Treat Yourself to Free Books and Free Gifts.

Answer 4 fun questions and get rewarded.

**We love to connect with our readers!
Please tell us a little about you...**

▶ DETACH AND MAIL CARD TODAY!

	YES	NO
1. I LOVE reading a good book.	○	○
2. I indulge and "treat" myself often.	○	○
3. I love getting FREE things.	○	○
4. Reading is one of my favorite activities.	○	○

TREAT YOURSELF • Pick your 2 Free Books...

Yes! Please send me my Free Books from each series I select and Free Mystery Gifts. I understand that I am under no obligation to buy anything, as explained on the back of this card.

Which do you prefer?
- ❏ **Love Inspired® Romance Larger-Print** 122/322 IDL GRDP
- ❏ **Love Inspired® Suspense Larger-Print** 107/307 IDL GRDP
- ❏ **Try Both** 122/322 & 107/307 IDL GRED

FIRST NAME

LAST NAME

ADDRESS

APT.#

CITY

STATE/PROV.

ZIP/POSTAL CODE

EMAIL ❏ Please check this box if you would like to receive newsletters and promotional emails from Harlequin Enterprises ULC and its affiliates. You can unsubscribe anytime.

LI/SLI-520-TY22

step forward to normalcy than it warranted. A big deal in a child's mind could easily turn into an object of fear.

"I think Moose would love to play ball with you."

Sophie scrambled off her lap. "Moose!" She ran across the porch and down the steps. "I'm coming! Daddy, it's my turn to play ball now."

Rob lowered the ball he'd been about to throw. "Okaaayyy…"

His eyes darted to Juliet, who'd come over to the steps. She gave him a small nod. "Sure, Sophie."

Raising the ball to shoulder height, in a perfect spiral with child-appropriate velocity, he tossed it to Sophie. She caught it like a pro.

Ambling closer, he ruffled her hair. "That's my girl. Good catch. Have fun."

Barking, Moose raced over to Sophie, and they went back to playing in the grass.

Rob joined Juliet at the steps, and she observed with concern the limp in his gait.

"You've been standing too much today. You need to sit and take the weight off your leg."

"Don't mind if I do." In one smooth motion, he dropped to the second top step. "How's your mom?" He motioned to the space beside him.

She sat down. "The procedure was pretty straight-forward. We should get the results next week. She was wiped out, though. Mom was resting on the sofa when I left her with Miss Evelyn."

Wincing a bit, he stretched out his long legs in front of him. "Doctor visits take their toll. White-coat syndrome." He leaned back on his elbows. "It's also exhausting watching someone you love going through it, too."

On the dresser in Sophie's room, there'd been a photo of Rob, toddler Sophie and a tall, pretty brunette.

Juliet hugged her knees. "Is that how you felt when Sophie's mother became sick?"

"Helpless might be more apt. And as you know, I'm not wired for inaction."

In his sigh, she heard the weight of his grief.

She swallowed. "Mom said it was leukemia."

"Cancer during pregnancy is rare, but it happens." He sat up. "It happened to Katrina." He looked at Sophie and Moose, but she knew it wasn't them he was seeing. "It happened to us."

"I'm so sorry, Rob."

"Because it doesn't happen that often, the data on treatment options is limited. She was in her third trimester when it was discovered. Balancing her health and the safety of the baby, the doctors advised delaying certain options until after the birth."

Juliet inched closer until her sleeve brushed his. Feeling helpless in the face of his pain.

His Adam's apple bobbed in his throat. "Unfortunately, in her case, it was too little, too late. Katrina was a fighter, but after a long struggle, she died when Sophie was not quite two." Hunching over, he rested his arms on his knees. "Saddest of all, Sophie doesn't even remember her mother."

Driven by the overwhelming urge to comfort him, she twined her arm around his. "I'm sorry for the pain you've experienced, too."

He leaned into her, hugging her arm. "You and I are kindred spirits, I think, when it comes to suffering."

"I used to wonder after Josh died—" she rested her chin on his bicep "—if a quick death versus a protracted death made any difference to the degree of grief."

He leaned his chin on the top of her head. "And what was your conclusion?"

"Pain is pain," she whispered into the crisp cotton of his sleeve.

They sat in silence for a while without the need for words. Under a bush, a robin trilled, bringing Juliet back from her own memories.

Blushing, she extricated herself. "Sorry," she rasped.

Rob frowned. "Don't be."

Her gaze ping-ponged to the houses on either side, and she wondered who'd witnessed her curling into him. That someone had witnessed it was never in doubt. This was Laurel Grove. And Miss Geraldine lived next door.

Someone had probably already called her mom. And hired skywriters to broadcast the news to the rest of the town.

Juliet shifted, uncomfortable, on the hard wooden step. She gestured. "Isn't it wonderful to see Sophie playing in the yard?" Her tone was bright, too bright.

"Juliet... We should talk about what just happened between us."

"There is no us." Facing him, she set her jaw. "And nothing just happened."

He shook his head. "That's not true. I felt it. I know you must've felt it, too."

This was her fault for getting carried away by the not-to-be-ignored charms of Rob Melbourne. And her stupid, adolescent crush on him. From the start, their banter had been flirty.

Which was totally unlike her. She'd never been a flirty type of girl. But like other things she didn't wish to examine too closely, he seemed to bring that out in her.

"What I felt—" She pursed her lips. "I'll grant you, we have some chemistry."

"Chemistry?" His eyes narrowed. "What we shared—"

"What we shared was empathy. Nothing more. And I apologize for my unprofessional conduct."

He scowled.

She lifted her chin. "A momentary lapse of judgment that mustn't be allowed to happen again."

"Lapse of judgment?" he growled.

"I'm sorry if I gave you the wrong impression." She was babbling again. But she couldn't seem to stop herself. "The fact of the matter is I'm not emotionally available for anything more. And I won't ever be."

A muscle ticked furiously in his jaw.

She couldn't look at him a moment longer. Desperate for somewhere else to land her gaze, she focused on the house next door, the lilac bush at the corner, the green lawn, before finally settling on Sophie and Moose.

The little girl had thrown the ball where it landed next to the hedge. At the edge of the grass, the yellow ball lay beside a long, curvy stick. Juliet squinted. Something didn't seem right.

"Get the ball, Moosie!" Sophie called.

But Moose growled, low and menacing. Juliet frowned. She'd never heard Moose make that noise before.

"Silly Moose." Sophie raced forward. "I'll get it myself."

Moose went into a frenzy of barking at the same moment the three-foot stick slithered in the grass and coiled.

Juliet jumped to her feet. "That's not a stick, Sophie!" she screamed, moving down the steps at a run. "Stop! Don't get any closer. Rob, don't let her—"

With a whoosh of air, he blew past her like she was standing still.

Chapter Nine

Rob flew across the lawn. But he knew he wasn't going to reach Sophie in time.

Just behind him, Juliet continued to shout Sophie's name. Reaching to grab the ball, Sophie spotted the copperhead and froze. Trapped against the hedge with nowhere to escape, the now tightly coiled snake vibrated its tail, ready to strike.

Help me, God.

With a burst of speed, he snatched his daughter into his arms. The snake lunged. Moose launched himself between Sophie and the copperhead.

The small dog's ferocious bark immediately turned into a high-pitched yelp.

"Moose!" Juliet dashed forward.

The shouting had brought the neighbors, Geraldine and her husband, Vernon, running. Rob set Sophie on her feet. Geraldine enveloped the little girl in her strong embrace.

"Stay back," Vernon yelled, carrying a large metal bucket. "Don't get too close, Juliet!"

Rob snagged Juliet around the waist, stopping her in her tracks.

"Let me go." She pushed against his hold. "I have to get to Moose."

He kept his arm around her. "Let Vernon deal with the snake first."

With a dexterous flip, Vernon managed to settle the bucket over the coiled snake. "Got anything heavy to put on top till we can get Animal Control out here, Rob?"

As soon as Rob let go of her, Juliet shot forward. She dropped to her knees in the grass. "Oh, Moose. What have you gotten yourself into now?"

The little dog whimpered. She stroked his head. Rob placed a heavy stone paver from the walkway on top of the bucket.

"Daddy?" Sophie's voice trembled. "Is Moose going to be all right?"

"Let me take a look." He exchanged a glance with Geraldine.

Nodding, the older woman put her arm around Sophie and drew her toward the steps.

Crouching beside Juliet, he performed a cursory examination of the dog.

Juliet's breath hitched. "His right front paw... Blood."

"I see it."

Two fang marks had broken the skin. The paw was also swollen and red.

He sat back on his heels. "Moose needs to go to the vet. Now."

She reached for the dog, but Rob stopped her.

"Careful."

"I... I should hold him." Her mouth trembled. "He'll want me to carry him."

"Of course, he will," Rob soothed. "Just let me get a blanket from the house to wrap him first. I'll lift him and hand him to you, I promise."

Blinking away tears, she nodded.

He bounded up the steps past Miss Geraldine and Sophie.

She caught hold of his leg. "Is Moose going to be all right, Daddy?"

His heart sank. Had the progress they made been undone? But he had no time to worry about that now. He had to make sure Moose got on his way to the vet as soon as possible. "I don't know, Soph."

Moose was such a tiny dog. It wouldn't take long for the venom traveling through his bloodstream to do irreparable damage. It might already be too late.

Dashing into the house, he grabbed a blanket from the wicker basket beside the couch and ran outside again.

He found a white-faced Juliet exactly where he'd left her. Vernon was on his cell phone. Gently, Rob lifted Moose, tucking the blanket around him.

Shaking like a beech leaf in a gale, Juliet rose. He placed the dog in her arms.

Vernon clicked off his phone. "Animal Control is on their way. Moose needs the vet." He eyed Rob. "Immediately."

"My keys," she murmured. "I'm not sure where I left " Lurching forward, she stumbled.

Rob steadied her. His heart was torn. "You shouldn't go alone. I'd drive you, but…" His eyes flickered toward the porch.

Holding Sophie's hand, Geraldine and his daughter ventured over. "Vernon and I can stay with Sophie."

"No!" Tearing free, Sophie glued herself to Juliet's side. "I want to go with Moose. I'm going to be brave for him."

Moose strained toward the sound of her voice.

Rob knelt beside his daughter. "Are you sure? We could be at the vet's a long time."

"Moose is my friend, Daddy. He's helped me so much. He needs me now." She hugged Juliet's dress. "Miss Juliet is sad. She needs us, too."

"All right. Let's get in my truck. I'll drive."

Vernon stuck his hands in his pockets. "I'll wait for Animal Control."

Geraldine nodded. "Don't worry about anything, Robbie. I'll lock the house." She patted Juliet's arm. "And start the prayer chain at church for Moose."

Juliet's eyes watered. "Do you think people in Laurel Grove will care about my little dog?"

Putting her arm around Juliet, Geraldine walked with her over to his truck parked alongside her car in the driveway. "People in Laurel Grove care about what concerns you. And so does God. Not the least of which is one little dog."

There was a flurry of activity as the three of them— it was kind of nice to think of them as a trio—got into his truck.

It didn't take but a minute to get to the veterinary clinic at the end of Main Street. Nothing was very far in Laurel Grove.

They hurried into the office. Moose was too quiet. It was late afternoon, near the close of the usual business day. They rushed to the counter.

Rob quickly explained the situation to the vet tech at the desk. The young man, one of Geraldine's nephews, put in a quick call to alert the vet. He ushered them past the swinging double doors into an examination room.

He gripped Sophie's hand. No one questioned him or Sophie following Juliet through. Which was good.

Because he had no intention of leaving Juliet to face this alone.

Seconds later, the veterinarian bustled into the room. She was new to the small-town practice. Very pretty in a blond way. And apparently, eligible. He knew this because the Knit-Knackers had been on a campaign to introduce them.

"Hi." She flashed them a quick smile, leaving him oddly unfazed. He and Sophie moved closer to Juliet.

"I'm Dr. Erickson. Is this Moose?"

Biting her lip, Juliet nodded.

Dr. Erickson's blue eyes were kind. "Please place him on the table so I can examine him."

Juliet laid the canine on the paper sheet. Moose whimpered. Sophie clung to Rob.

The vet performed a quick exam. "What happened exactly?" She restrung the stethoscope around her neck.

Her breath shuddery, Juliet gave her a brief account of what had transpired.

Dr. Erickson continued to check out the wound on Moose's swollen paw. "You're sure it was a copperhead?"

Juliet looked at Rob.

"Yes, ma'am," he spoke up. "It was a copperhead."

The vet smiled at him. "Rob Melbourne? I saw your picture in the paper. I know your aunt."

Glowering, Sophie inserted herself between him and the table. She twined one arm around him and the other arm around Juliet.

Juliet wrung her hands. "It happened so fast. We brought Moose here as quick as we could."

Dr. Erickson placed her hand on Moose's head. "You did the right thing. And you stayed calm. If you're calm, your pet is more likely to stay calm. The calmer Moose stays, the slower the venom distribution."

The vet was extremely pretty. But again, it left him indifferent. Quivering, Juliet appeared forlorn. He put an arm around her shoulders.

"I want to run a few tests and clean the wound." Dr. Erickson motioned toward the door. "If you'll wait in the reception area, I'll soon have a better idea of Moose's prognosis."

"But…" Juliet's anguished gaze swept from Moose to Rob.

Taking her arm, he leaned close to her ear. "We need to let the doc work, sweetheart."

She allowed him to lead her from the room without further protest. As they exited, Moose didn't make a sound. The vet tech met them with a clipboard of papers to fill out.

Finally, they retreated to the waiting area.

"It wasn't like Moose to be so quiet." Juliet sank onto the padded bench. "Do you think that means he's fading?" She knotted her hands.

He sat beside her, pulling Sophie onto his lap. "We shouldn't jump to conclusions. Let's wait to hear what the vet says about his condition."

She clenched and unclenched her hands. "If anything happens to Moose, I don't know what I'll do."

"Cry if you want to." Feeling an overwhelming need to offer comfort, to touch her, he rested his shoulder against hers. "It will make you feel better."

She shook her head. "It won't."

"Tears wash away the hurt."

"Hasn't worked for me thus far." She looked at him. "I've never been one to make a public display."

Rob understood that about her. Concerning the deep things in her heart, she was a very private person. Perhaps if she were less so, she would be less consumed still by the death of her husband. Everyone had to find their own path through grief, but he ached for the pain she carried inside. And now this?

Slipping off his lap, Sophie leaned against Juliet's knees. "I'm sorry, Miss Juliet." His daughter's voice sounded thick with unshed tears. "I... I never meant for Moose to get hurt."

"Oh, darling." Juliet opened her arms. "This wasn't your fault." She brought Sophie into her lap.

"Is Moose going to die?" Sobbing, Sophie buried her face in Juliet's shoulder. "My m-mommy died when I was little. I miss her so much. Everyone at school has a mommy, except for me."

Stunned, he sat back suddenly.

His daughter twined her arms around Juliet's neck. "Today was such a happy day and then... And then..."

Juliet hugged her tightly. "There are sometimes snakes in the garden of the happiest days." Concern in her gaze, she glanced at him.

Leukemia. War. An innocent trip to the store. Stuff happened.

Juliet stroked his daughter's back in a soothing, circular motion. "But happier days will come again."

Sophie lifted her head. "Are you sure?"

He held his breath, wondering how she would answer. Juliet's grief was so palpable, just beneath the surface.

She smiled at his child. "I'm sure of it. Sometimes when we least expect it." She gave him a wobbly smile, but a smile all the same.

He took her hand, lacing his fingers through hers, and she didn't pull away.

Gradually, Sophie's sobs subsided. Tucking her head underneath Juliet's chin, her breathing slowed, becoming more even. "I love you, Miss Juliet."

Juliet's mouth quivered. "I… I love you, too, Sophie."

Her words touched a deep chord inside Rob. After Katrina died, he believed he'd never experience that again.

With her arms curled around Juliet, Sophie drifted off to sleep, worn out by the day's events.

"Are you okay?" Juliet squeezed his hand. "What Sophie said about her mother…"

He scrubbed his face. "I thought she didn't remember Katrina."

"Perhaps it isn't Katrina she misses as much as not having a mother."

Rob swallowed. "I've been naive to believe I could make up for that kind of loss in her life."

Had he been wrong about everything else, too?

"You're a wonderful father, Rob," Juliet whispered. "But Sophie's admission gives me new insight into why she reacted as she did after the shooting."

"What do you mean?"

"The loss of her mother, compounded with seeing her beloved father injured in the shooting, terrified her that she might lose the only parent she had left."

It gutted him to think of his baby girl struggling with such fears. Maybe Aunt Evie and her friends hadn't been so far off the mark in pushing him to remarry and find a new mother for his daughter.

Watching his sleeping child comforted in Juliet's arms, he was taken aback by the intensity of his feelings for her. Was he falling in love with Juliet Newkirk? They'd only become reacquainted a few days ago. After the sadness of losing Katrina, God had brought this wonderful woman into his and Sophie's lives. Was Juliet his second chance for happiness?

But unlike him, in her journey toward healing, Juliet wasn't ready to embrace a new beginning. Not yet anyway. But more than ever, he was convinced she did feel something for him.

More than she could even admit to herself. She'd made room in her heart for a tiny dog and for his daughter. Might one day she find room there for him, too?

Dr. Erickson bustled through the swinging double doors.

Getting to his feet, he took the sleeping Sophie from Juliet. Dread in her eyes, Juliet rose. Together they faced the veterinarian. Time for the verdict on Moose. His gut tightened.

She'd suffered so much loss in her life. *Dear God, please not another.*

Heart thundering, Juliet clasped her hands under her chin. *You see the tiniest sparrow. Please help my little dog to be all right.* It had been long time. Would God still hear her prayers?

The vet faced them. "Good news. The copperhead inflicted what is known as a 'dry bite' on Moose."

Shifting Sophie to the crook of his arm, Rob placed his other arm around Juliet. "That is good news."

Juliet looked from him to the vet. "I don't understand."

"A dry bite doesn't release venom." Dr. Erickson smiled. "Copperheads are known for giving what is essentially a warning bite. Good thing Moose didn't tangle with a diamondback."

Juliet released a slow breath. "What does this mean for Moose?"

"When no envenomization occurs, we treat the bite as a puncture wound only. Most swelling resolves within forty-eight hours. I've given Moose an antibiotic and an anti-inflammatory to be on the safe side. And also, an antihistamine for his comfort."

Juliet put her hand to her throat. "Will Moose suffer any long-term complications?"

Dr. Erickson shook her cap of glossy blond hair. "We'd be having a different conversation if he had been injected with venom. The location of the bite on his paw versus his head is in his favor. And you got him medical attention right away. But owing to his small size..."

Juliet took a ragged breath. "The venom would have spread rapidly throughout his small body."

"For the next twenty-four hours, I'd like Moose to remain here for observation." Dr. Erickson touched Juliet's sleeve. "I'm just being cautious. No real worries."

Juliet nodded. "Whatever you think is best. Thank you for your help. Can I say goodbye?"

"He's groggy. Give us a call in the morning, and I'll let you know how he fared overnight."

Juliet breathed a silent prayer of gratitude to God.

Rob stuck out his hand. "Thank you so much, Dr. Erickson, for taking good care of our little buddy."

The tall, coolly beautiful veterinarian flashed him a brilliant smile. "Please call me Ingrid."

With her nagging worry over Moose relieved, Juliet suddenly noticed how gorgeous the veterinarian truly was. And the inordinate amount of interest she appeared to show in Rob. Irritated, Juliet tapped her foot on the linoleum.

Ingrid Erickson held on to Rob's hand a little longer than Juliet believed necessary. So unprofessional in her opinion.

Not that he appeared to mind the attention. He smiled at the vet. Juliet's mouth flattened.

Could he not see the doctor was attracted to him? That charm of his was as natural as breathing. Same old story since kindergarten. Women falling at his feet. And he was clueless.

She propped her hands on her hips.

"I've been wanting to meet you. Such a hero." Ingrid Erickson threw Rob's bicep an admiring glance.

Juliet went rigid. His smile faded a tad.

"Moose was the hero today." He extricated his hand from the veterinarian. "He saved my daughter from the snake."

Erickson's smile never faltered. "I'd love the chance for us to get to know each other better."

"Uh… Umm…" Eyes wide, his gaze flicked to Juliet.

Taking pity on him, she looped her arm around his. "We should get Sophie home. It's been a tiring day."

"Oh." Ingrid Erickson's face fell. "Of course."

With Sophie propped against his shoulder, Juliet steered them to the parking lot.

"Thanks for the save, Jules."

She smacked his arm. "Let that be a lesson to you to keep your powers under better control."

"Excuse me, my what?"

She fluttered her hand. "The smile. The charm. The face. Use at your own risk."

"You don't like my face?"

She opened her mouth, thought better of it and closed it. *If only that were true.*

He clicked his key fob. "But my smile doesn't seem to have much effect on you." He opened the door.

She tucked a strand of hair behind her ear. "I told you I'm completely immune to your powers." *Liar.*

"Don't hold back, Jules." He grimaced. "Tell me how you really feel."

He gently lowered the sleeping Sophie into her booster

seat. "I wasn't sure how to turn the vet down without hurting her feelings."

"You were going to turn her down?"

He clicked the booster seat belt in place and straightened. "She's not my type."

"What is your type?" As soon as the words left her mouth, she would've done anything to call them back. "I mean... Not that it's any of my—"

"I prefer brunettes. With big brown eyes." He shut the door with a soft click.

Juliet's heart clamored. Was he referring to her?

Rob leaned against the truck, stretching his jean-clad legs in front of him. Her pulse raced. He folded his arms across his chest and gave her a look.

Cheeks warming, she fanned her face. "The humidity today is really something."

"I hadn't noticed." He cut his gaze to her. "Thanks for the heads-up about my 'powers' as you called them."

She rolled her eyes. "You're welcome."

"It's a shame how some women only focus on the external." He pulled a tragic face. "Makes a guy feel so objectified."

She laughed. So hard she fell against the truck. So loud, she covered her mouth before she woke Sophie.

Rob threw her a lopsided grin.

"How terrible it must be to be you." She smirked.

"Well..." He opened his hands. "There is that." He gave her a teasing look. "But it's good to see you smile again. And laugh."

She'd laughed more in the last few days than she had in years. With a sudden jolt, she remembered that earlier he'd called her *sweetheart*. Coming from him, it was an endearment it would be far too easy to become accustomed to.

Best not to let him know the knee-wobbling effect he had on her sensibilities. That wouldn't do. It wouldn't do at all.

Rob wasn't sure what had triggered her sudden silence. She'd gone quiet. Too quiet.

Or maybe whatever it was he'd said or done had gotten too close. Too real for the cocoon in which she'd apparently decided to spend the rest of her life.

Was it forever to be one step forward with this woman and two steps back? Doubts overwhelmed him. What was the point in beating his head against the proverbial brick wall with her?

"Thank you so much for helping me get Moose to the vet. And being there for me." Her gaze locked with his.

For a split second, he thought…he hoped… His heart surged.

Then, suddenly shuttering her expression, Juliet smoothed her khaki skirt. "I should check on my mom."

Withholding a sigh, he opened the passenger door. "Right." He held out his hand to assist her into the truck.

Hesitating, her eyes flitted to his.

"I thought you were immune to my so-called powers?"

She lifted her chin. "I am." Taking his hand, she stepped up into the truck.

"Ouch," he winced. "I can always count on you to keep my ego in check."

She batted those chocolate-brown eyes of hers at him. "Think of it as a public service. Courtesy of Paw Pals. Part of the whole body, therapy package."

He smiled all the way back to his house. He figured she'd dash away as soon as he pulled into the driveway, but as always, she surprised him.

She insisted on helping him get Sophie inside. Taking

the key from him, she went ahead to open the door while he carefully gathered his sleeping child into his arms.

A movement over the hedge caught his eye. Sitting in the swing on their own porch, Geraldine and Vernon waved. They'd want a report on Moose.

He made a motion as if holding a phone to his ear, but Geraldine shook her head. Vernon gave him a big thumbs-up.

The Laurel Grove grapevine had struck again. The vet-tech nephew. Miss Geraldine was nothing if not resourceful. And a great neighbor.

Juliet closed the door behind him. "Bedroom?" she mouthed.

He nodded. She hurried ahead to Sophie's bedroom to turn down the bedspread. Stooping, he laid his small daughter on her pink-infatuated bed.

Juliet gently eased off Sophie's white sandals. With a contented sigh, his little girl turned over onto her side.

He and Juliet exchanged anxious looks, holding their collective breath. But tucking her hands under her chin, Sophie never opened her eyes.

Juliet brushed a tendril of hair out of Sophie's face, fanning it over the pillow. There was such a gut-wrenching look in her eyes. And he grieved with her for the child she'd lost. The child she never had the chance to know.

But straightening, she tiptoed out of the room. He followed, leaving the door ajar.

She picked up Moose's backpack, and yet she lingered. Perhaps as reluctant as he to end their time together. Or was that him just hoping again?

"You couldn't save your own child, so you save other people's children instead."

Her lips trembled. "Yes." She darted a glance at Sophie's door. "She's emotionally exhausted. Maybe she'll sleep through the night."

Rob ran his hand over his head. "I wish I could believe that."

"Tomorrow I may have something we could try— Oh." Her lovely mouth rounded. "I won't have Moose. Should I come anyway? Just me?"

"Just you is just perfect."

He took the backpack from her, and they moved out onto the porch. The afternoon was gone. The languid summer evening was upon them.

The sun was low on the horizon, painting the sky in broad swaths of apricot, pink and lavender. Tummy rumbling, Sophie would soon awaken, wanting her dinner. Would there be more tears over the fright she'd had earlier?

He pursed his lips. "Do you think this latest trauma with Moose will destroy the gains we've made?"

"Going to the vet was a big step forward for Sophie." Juliet sighed. "I think she's on the mend. She just needs a little more time and a whole lot of love."

Is that what Juliet needed, too? A little more time and a whole lot of love?

"Why are we whispering?" he whispered.

She gave him a tremulous smile. "Does it seem to you that many of our conversations have been whispered?"

"Now that you mention it, yes. The hazards of single parenting. Sophie is always with me."

Smiling, she took the backpack from him. "Don't pretend you mind. You adore her. And so do I."

His daughter wasn't the only one exhausted by the events of the day. None more so than Juliet, who'd started her day by taking her mom for a biopsy. Time to steer the conversation into an area less fraught with emotion.

Folding his arms, he propped against one of the porch posts. "Thanks again for the rescue with the vet." He made a show of rubbing the stubble on his face. "Although, it was nice to know someone finds me appealing. Unlike you." He gave her the best version of his crooked grin.

She looked up at him quickly and then down again. "I never said I didn't find you appealing." She placed her palm against his cheek.

He melted against her hand.

Mouth curving, she pulled away. "In a totally ridiculous sort of way, of course." Sauntering down the steps toward her car, she laughed.

He grinned. A good detective learned early to read body language. He was beginning to understand how to read the lovely dog handler.

Juliet Mitchell Newkirk liked him. No matter what she said or didn't say. She liked him. A lot.

Not as much as he liked her. Not yet... Now he had only to convince Juliet to give him a chance.

Chapter Ten

The next morning, Juliet lugged the plastic bin up the walkway to the Melbournes's porch. Rob and Sophie came out to greet her.

Juliet set the bin on the step. Sophie hugged her. She loved the feel of Sophie's arms around her waist.

He took the bin. "Let me carry that for you."

"Such a gentleman. Thank you." She made sure to catch his eye. "Robbie."

He groaned. "You heard that? To Miss Geraldine, I'll always be about seventeen."

"I don't miss much." She moistened her lips. "Robbie."

He hefted the bin in his strong arms. "I noticed that about you in high school, Miss Most Likely to Someday Rule the World. How's Moose?"

"I called this morning. He rested comfortably last night. Dr. Erickson has signed off for me to pick him up later today."

"Good news." Rob smiled the smile that made her knees wobble.

"What's in the box, Miss Juliet?" Sophie bounced up and down like a pogo stick. "Is it for me? Is it a present?"

He frowned. "Sophie!"

Juliet slipped an arm around Sophie's shoulders. The three of them went inside. "It absolutely is for Sophie. Mom and I put it together last night as a surprise."

"What is it? What is it?"

Juliet smiled at her exuberance. "My old dress-up box. It's such a lovely morning. We could look through everything on the screened porch and get some fresh air at the same time."

Sophie clasped her hands under her chin. "Can I try on stuff?"

Juliet opened her hands. "What else is a dress-up box for, if not to put on hats, gloves, jewelry and high heels?"

He set the bin on the table in the screened porch. "Count me out." He turned back toward the kitchen.

Juliet chewed her lip. "You don't have to go, Rob."

"Yes, he does." Sophie propped her hands on her small hips. "This isn't for daddies."

"Ouch." He put his hand on his heart. "I know where I'm not wanted."

That wasn't how she felt at all. On the contrary, increasingly she found herself wanting to be with him.

She'd done a lot of thinking last night. Evaluating Sophie's progress. Recalibrating the therapy schedule. And owning her attraction to Rob.

The first step in any recovery process was to admit she had a problem. Then, work the problem for a solution. Same way she'd tackled every dilemma since high school—by taking control of the situation. She'd implement the same plan she'd utilized with Sophie—exposure therapy.

Surely overfamiliarity would mitigate the butterfly-fluttery arrhythmia he produced in her heart. But in the meantime, there was no harm in enjoying his friendship. Was there?

Why not enjoy every moment she could with them?

He winked. "I'm sure I can find something to occupy myself." He made a face. "Like doing my PT. But I wouldn't mind a fashion show after you ladies get decked out."

Wrenching off the box lid, Sophie had stopped listening. Amid oohs and aahs of delight, she started rummaging.

Juliet lowered her voice. "I also talked to the hospital counselor this morning. Mrs. Larsen is thrilled about Sophie's breakthrough. We think Sophie will be ready to meet with her next week. Hopefully, that also means you'll be able to resume your PT and return to work."

"Next week?" He scowled. "You're that eager to be rid of us, are you? To hand us off to Mrs. Larsen and leave Laurel Grove?"

She reared a fraction. "Actually, I plan to stick around Laurel Grove at least another week. To be with Mom when she gets her biopsy results. And help Sophie tick off the items on her Being Brave list. I thought you'd be pleased."

"I am." He ran his hand through his short-cropped hair, leaving it rumpled and sticking straight up. "Sorry."

"Another late night?"

He glanced over to Sophie, who was busy winding colorful scarves around her neck. "I have some job-related concerns on my mind, too."

The little girl looked at them. "Will Moose be able to come and play today?"

"Not today." Juliet sat down at the table. "The vet says Moose needs to take it easy for the next couple of days."

Rob pulled out a chair. "It's the little dog with the big heart's turn to be the patient."

She gave the chair a sidelong look. "What happened to doing PT?"

"Can't let you have all the fun without me. Plus, I don't want to deprive you ladies of my company."

She rolled her eyes. "So considerate of you."

He grinned. "I try."

They spent the next hour sorting through the box and donning costumes. Juliet chose a feather boa, glittery flapper beads and a headband.

And Sophie declared her dad hilarious when he tried on a fedora that once belonged to Juliet's grandfather.

Be still my heart. It gave him a kind of globe-trotting, treasure hunter vibe. Leave it to Rob to somehow manage to become even more rakishly handsome.

And because she was so confident in her new plan—in her resolve to enjoy Rob's friendship—when he asked her to eat lunch with them, she accepted with pleasure.

But later, she reluctantly declined the opportunity to ride to the farm and check off another item on Sophie's Being Brave list.

Juliet scraped the lunch plates and stacked them. "I'm supposed to pick up Moose from the vet soon."

Sophie gathered the silverware into a bundle. "He'll be so happy to see you."

Juliet smiled. "And Fluff-Fluff, too."

"I wish I had a dog." Sophie handed the utensils to her father. "Don't you wish we had a dog like Moose, Daddy?"

He loaded the silverware in the dishwasher. "There's not many dogs like Moose."

Juliet rinsed off a plate. "It takes a special dog with very specific traits to be a great therapy dog." She handed the plate to Rob.

On the other side of the island, Sophie climbed onto the stool. "Like what?"

Juliet handed him the last plate to stack. "Not every dog is comfortable being petted. When we go visit patients in the hospital or in nursing homes or even make school visits, that's part of Moose's job."

"Daddy." Sophie put her hands around her mouth to whisper. "Did you ask Miss Juliet about Moose going to my school?"

"Why don't you ask her yourself?" he whispered back.

Juliet chuckled. "Since I can hear both of you perfectly well, I think something can be arranged."

"Yay!" Sophie fist-pumped the air. "What else, Miss Juliet? What else about Moose's specialness?"

"Let's see." She leaned against the countertop. "Therapy dogs stay calm, even when there are loud noises." She tapped her finger on her chin, thinking out loud. "They have happy, sunny personalities."

Sophie perked. "Moose is such a happy dog."

"He enjoys his work."

Rob propped his elbow on the counter. "Enjoying the work is a huge deal."

Somehow, she got the feeling he'd stopped talking about Moose. She made a mental note to ask him what he meant later. "One more thing."

"What?" Sophie's eyes widened.

"Therapy dogs have good manners."

"I have good manners."

"You do." Rob tweaked her nose. "But you're not a therapy dog, Soph."

Juliet loved watching the two of them.

"I had to teach Moose to obey certain commands like drop it or leave it. To sit. To walk on a leash. To come when called." Juliet sighed. "I think Moose found his true calling in therapy work. I know I sure did."

Rob straightened. "Did you go looking for a potential therapy dog at the rescue shelter?"

Juliet eased onto the bar stool beside Sophie. "Moose found me. Even when he was a puppy, I realized how remarkable he was." She shrugged. "The calling sort of found us both."

Soon after, they headed out. Rob and Sophie went to the farm. But receiving a text from her mom, Juliet diverted to the knitting shop.

At the store, she pushed open the door. The bell jangled overhead. The twenty-something assistant manager waved before helping an older woman with her yarn selection.

Her mom stepped out of her office. "Hi, darling. Thanks for stopping by." She held up the mini-Moose stuffed toy. "Voilà!"

"Oh, Mom." Juliet examined it. "It's just like him. It's so cute. Adorable."

Her mother smiled. "I thought it turned out well."

"Sophie is going to love it." She hugged her mom. "I love it."

"The Knit-Knack gals loved it, too." Her mother tilted her head. "In fact, what would you think of having multiple mini-Mooses to share with the children you work with through Paw Pals? The girls are itching to find another long-term project. Have yarn, must craft."

Juliet's heart quickened. "To be able to give one to each child would be wonderful. And such a good idea." She squeezed her mom's hand. "Not only providing comfort— I think it would also prove beneficial to their recovery."

"Great. We'll get right on—" Her mother's eyes narrowed. "You're glowing."

She flushed. "I'm not glowing."

Her mother gave her a skeptical look. "I might even go so far as to say you're radiant. Time with Rob seems to agree with you."

"Time with Sophie," she corrected. "If I'm feeling especially happy it's because Sophie is doing so well. Because I'm about to pick up Moose. And thanks to you…" She held up the mini-Moose.

"Whatever you say," her mother smirked.

Juliet cut her eyes at the clock. "Would you look at the time? Gotta go. Don't want to keep Moose waiting."

"By all means, don't keep my favorite pup waiting." Her mother waved her off. "Try and hide if you can, but it looks like love has already found you."

Rolling her eyes, she headed for the door. "See you at dinner."

Moose was ecstatic to see her. It wasn't long after getting him settled at her mom's house that she received a message from Rob. Thinking of you.

He was all she'd been thinking of, too.

Face flaming, she was glad her mother wasn't there. She'd have never heard the end of it. But she remembered her resolve to enjoy the present. She'd only be in Laurel Grove another week.

Before she lost her nerve, she texted back. Thinking of you, too. As soon as she hit Send, she could feel her neck redden.

There was an immediate response. How's Moose?

Safer terrain. Breathing a sigh of relief, she gave him the pertinent details. Then texted, How's Sophie?

He replied that she was coping well with the visit to the farm. Is Moose up for a short visit? We could swing by. I miss you.

Her lips curved. She missed him, too. Not that she

was about to admit that to him. Why was it that even a text from him made her feel so happy? You saw me 3 hours ago.

His response: You're a very missable person. You don't want to see us?

Come on over. I have a mini-Moose for Soph. What's your ETA?

When it comes to you, I live ever hopeful.

A smiley emoji. Then, he texted: Pulling into your neighborhood now.

With a shriek, she threw her cell onto the bed and jumped up. He couldn't see her like this. Her clothes were rumpled from snuggling with Moose. And her hair was a mess.

She dashed into the bathroom.

From his doggie bed in the corner of her room, Moose raised his head.

She had only time to run a brush through her hair. The doorbell rang. Her heart went into overdrive. Moose barked.

Juliet scooped up her dog. *Why are you running? Slow down. It's just old friend Rob. No big deal.*

She threw open the door.

"Hey there! Long time, no see." Blue eyes twinkling, he grinned at her.

She melted, more than a little. "Hey, yourself."

Behind him, Sophie amused herself by jumping from one step to another. "Hey, Moose. Hey, Miss Juliet."

Juliet's gaze locked with his. A surge of sheer pleasure shot through her. Irrational. Idiotic. Undeniable.

And she was forced to acknowledge he'd become more than just a friend.

Yet for the life of her, she couldn't find the strength to mind.

Rob smiled. "Moose seems to be feeling more like his old self." He glanced around Lesley Mitchell's living room.

Crouching on the area rug, Sophie played with the small dog.

"He's limping only slightly." Juliet rummaged through her purse on the table in the foyer. She drew out the tiny stuffed Moose replica.

"Wow! Too cool. Your mom nailed Moose." He grinned. "Right down to the bat ears."

She swatted at him. "Hush."

They walked over to the sofa and sat down.

Juliet hid the stuffed animal behind a pillow. "Could you come over here for a minute, Sophie? My mom made something for you."

"Your mommy made something for me?" Bouncing up, Sophie joined them. "Where is it?"

Juliet pulled the toy from behind the pillow. "Ta-da!"

"It's— " Sophie's eyes went large. "Daddy, it looks just like Moose."

He chuckled. "I know."

"Thank you, Miss Juliet." Sophie clutched the soft, cuddly animal to her chest. "I love it."

"You're so welcome, sweet girl." She planted a quick kiss on Sophie's forehead. "Now you can have your very own Moose."

It made him proud he didn't have to prompt her to thank Juliet for the gift.

Juliet snuggled Sophie against her side. "I understand you've been having a hard time sleeping at night."

Sophie bit her lip. "I wake up and get scared thinking about my daddy getting hurt."

He slid forward. "I'm doing good now, Soph. There's no need to worry about me anymore."

"It was a scary experience, though, wasn't it?" Juliet gazed into Sophie's eyes. "I'm hoping mini-Moose might help you not be so afraid the next time you wake up in the middle of the night. Can we try an experiment?"

Sophie nodded.

"You'll need to lie down."

Sophie dropped to the rug. "Should I 'tend like I'm asleep, Miss Juliet?"

He winked at Juliet. "I think you should, Soph." He handed his daughter a couch cushion.

Flopping dramatically onto the pillow, Sophie closed her eyes and let out an enormous snore. Her eyes flew open and she giggled. "I'm so silly, Miss Juliet."

Juliet shook her head. "The silliest child in the world."

Sophie giggled again.

Juliet placed the toy on Sophie's chest. "When you wake up, do the exercises I showed you. Watch mini-Moose go up and down with your breathing."

Sophie practiced a few times.

"Excellent as always." She gathered Sophie up in her arms. "Will you promise to try this if you wake up tonight?"

"I'll try for you, Miss Juliet."

Juliet kissed her head. "You are the best, Sophie."

"And you are the best Miss Juliet ever."

Juliet's lips curved. "Why thank you, darling. That's one of the nicest things anyone has ever said to me."

He rose. "We should go, Soph, so Miss Juliet and her mom can have dinner."

Sophie made a face. "I didn't get to thank Miss Lesley for making mini-Moose for me."

"That's right. So you should stay." Juliet smiled. "Have dinner with us."

"Are you sure? I don't want to impose." He sniffed the air appreciatively. "But by any chance, is that pot roast I smell?"

Juliet motioned him to sit again. "It's been in the slow cooker since this morning, and you're not imposing. I invited you."

"I'm not one to turn down a home-cooked meal." Nor a chance to spend more time with Juliet. "We accept with pleasure."

Lesley arrived not long after. Sophie made him proud again by thanking Juliet's mother for the stuffed animal.

After dinner, Lesley wanted to send them home with a bouquet of flowers from her garden. Sophie tagged along to help her cut them. Which gave him and Juliet a few moments alone.

Rob took hold of her hand. "Thank you for everything, Juliet."

Her heart skipped a beat. "I hope both of you get a full night's sleep."

Rob brushed his lips across the back of her hand. "Me, too."

Her gaze held his for a breathless moment. Sophie and Lesley rejoined them. With reluctance, Rob let go of her hand. But the memory of Juliet's smile stayed with him long after he reached home.

The next morning, Rob was waiting on the porch with an extra cup of coffee when Juliet pulled into his driveway.

Getting out of her car, she hurried over. "How did it go last night?" Tucked into the crook of her arm, Moose's tail swished.

Rob took the backpack off her shoulder and handed her the mug.

She frowned. "Does this mean it was another sleepless night?"

"Quite the contrary." He raised his mug. "Here's to you, Juliet Newkirk, therapy dog handler extraordinaire. I heard Sophie wake up at about 3:00 a.m., but I didn't rush in. I watched from the hall. She went through the breathing exercises, tucked mini-Moose under her chin and promptly went back to sleep."

Hearing a version of his name, Moose barked.

Juliet exhaled. "That's wonderful. I'm so relieved."

He took Moose from her. The tiny dog licked his chin. "Coulda done without that, little dude, but many thanks to you, too, for helping Sophie."

"Where is my favorite little girl?" Juliet clicked mugs with him. "I can't wait to congratulate her."

He grinned. "She's getting dressed to tackle the next item on her Brave list."

Juliet shook her head. "She wants to go to the ice cream store? Now?"

"Doors open at ten." Out of habit, he rested his hand on his hip where his gun belt usually rode. "Care to join us?"

She batted her lashes at him. "When you know me better, you'll know this girl doesn't turn down ice cream any time of the day."

"You said, 'when I know you better' not 'if.'" He smiled. "Seems like I'm growing on you." He took a sip of coffee.

"Sure you are." She gave him a side-glance. "Like fungus."

He spluttered into his coffee and grinned. The day had the makings of a wonderful day. And it was.

The next few days, he and Juliet spent a lot of time together, getting to know each other. Over the weekend, they took a picnic and went hiking at nearby Hanging Rock State Park with Sophie and Moose.

On Tuesday, Juliet accompanied them to Sophie's appointment with Mrs. Larsen at the hospital. Her mom graciously allowed Moose to spend the day with her at the Ewe.

The counselor told them to call her if symptoms reemerged, but she didn't feel further visits were warranted.

While in Greensboro, Juliet took Sophie shopping. "Can't have her terrified to go into a big-box store for the rest of her life. Think how her wardrobe would suffer."

Rob had been nervous, but Sophie did fine. No fear going into the store or of being in a crowd.

In the children's department, Juliet picked out a frilly, pink dress for Sophie to try on. "We have to celebrate Sophie achieving the milestones on her Brave list."

Sophie adored the dress. "I look so bee-you-ti-ful." She twirled around and around in front of the mirror, letting the pleated folds of the dress swirl. "Do you think I look bee-you-ti-ful, Daddy?"

At her happiness, tears misted his eyes. "You look so…" His voice clogged.

Juliet hugged his daughter. "You look so lovely you've made your daddy speechless." She threw him a teasing look. "When Mr. Charming goes quiet, that is *quite* the feat."

Rob nudged her. "Similar to the effect you have on me, too."

Juliet pursed her lips, but he could tell his words pleased her. "You realize a dress this fabulous requires matching shoes."

He groaned. "What have you gotten me into, Newkirk?"

"Girls are expensive, Melbourne." She tapped the end of his nose. "Better get used to it."

Juliet bought the dress for Sophie before he could stop her.

She held up her hand. "My treat. Don't spoil my joy. I'll let you buy the shoes, though."

After dinner at a Mexican restaurant, they drove back to Laurel Grove, and he dropped Juliet at her mom's. He put Sophie to bed. Mini-Moose occupied a permanent spot on her pillow.

He and Sophie prayed together. Then, he tucked the covers around her.

"I wish Miss Juliet and Moose could stay with us forever. I wish she could be my mommy," Sophie whispered.

His breath hitched at the image of the three of them as a family. The depth of yearning in his heart for Juliet to become a part of his life caught him by surprise. But there was a rightness to it.

"I pray every night for her to love us, Daddy."

"She already loves you." He kissed her forehead. "And I appreciate your prayers on my behalf."

Other than the trip to Greensboro, they took Moose on the majority of their adventures. Juliet claimed Moose whined unless he got his daily dose of Sophie. Miss Lesley was good about keeping Moose at her house in the evenings so Rob and Juliet could spend time together after Sophie went to bed.

They'd hang out on the porch, enjoying the gardenia-scented night air and each other. Sharing childhood memories. And personal preferences from everything like anchovies on pizza (hers) to blue corn chips (his).

Small, inconsequential things really, but the kind of stuff that made up a life.

Each evening, there'd be tons of muffled laughter with

Juliet shushing him so as to not wake the neighbors or Sophie. Until she'd declare they'd scandalized Laurel Grove long enough and she'd head home. Only to call him when she arrived. Their phone conversations sometimes lasted a few more hours.

Eventually, the lighthearted banter they did so well gave way to deeper topics. Her dream for Paw Pals. His doubts about returning to the Greensboro PD. He told her about his life with Katrina, and how good God had been to him both during her illness and after her death.

On Thursday night, while on the phone, she finally reciprocated by telling him about how she and Josh had met. About their courtship. The years she pursued advanced degrees as they moved from one Marine base to another. Perhaps she found it easier to share these things over the phone.

The entire time he remained silent, understanding what a gift it was—this glimpse into her heart. Afraid to interrupt. Afraid to stop the flow of her recollections.

She didn't talk about Josh's death, and he didn't push. For now, it was enough. He was gratified she'd trusted him with these most tender of memories.

But the more he learned about Juliet, the more he wanted to know. The more he became sure what he was feeling for her was real and true.

He was well aware he was living on borrowed time with her. Any day now her mom would get the results from her biopsy, and Juliet's last reason to remain in Laurel Grove would vanish.

Would he and Sophie be reason enough to stay?

Chapter Eleven

Friday morning got off to a rocky start. Juliet's mom left to open the store, but returned a few minutes later.

Juliet glanced up from buttering her toast. "Did you forget something?"

"Looks like it's going to be one of those days…" Her mother laid her keys on the granite countertop. "My car won't start."

Juliet put down the butter knife. "Do you need me to run you to the Ewe?"

"If it wouldn't be too much trouble." Her mom readjusted the knitting tote on her shoulder. "I hope that won't interfere with your plans with Rob."

Juliet arched her brow. "You're assuming I have plans with Rob."

"Don't you?"

"Well, yes. I do." Juliet's lips twitched. "With Rob *and* Sophie, but not till later."

"Thought so, but I'd appreciate a lift if you can fit me into your schedule."

She gave her mother a quick peck on the cheek. "For you, anything."

"Finish your toast." Her mom took out her phone. "I'll

call my mechanic to stop by and check out what's wrong with the car. I'll leave the keys under the mat for him."

Juliet shook her head. Unlocked, and keys under the mat. Only in Laurel Grove.

The mechanic was a longtime friend who lived down the block, and neighbors helped neighbors. Small-town life had its perks. And thinking of Rob—as she was wont to do all hours of the day and night—Laurel Grove had an abundance of charm.

Juliet left Moose in his crate. After dropping her mother off at the shop, she drove down Main Street, taking stock of the recent changes in her hometown.

She waved at an old high school friend, who was now proprietor of her own fashionable boutique. There was also a new bakery in town. The historic train depot was undergoing a renovation, too. Downtown was making a comeback.

Once they'd heard she was in town, friends had been calling or stopping by all week. It had been great to reconnect. The pace of small-town life was growing on her. Or was that just Rob?

Spotting a real estate sign in the window of a long-unoccupied storefront, she slowed the car to a crawl. *Huh.* The old Whitaker building.

Giving in to the impulse, she pulled to the curb in front of the two-story brick building. Unable to resist taking a peek, she strolled over to the large window to take a look inside.

Her granddad had been one of the driving forces on the historic preservation committee, and her mom had continued his work to revitalize Laurel Grove. The Whitaker building had once housed an emporium before large shopping centers sprang up on the highway and lured local customers away. Often dragged to boring planning meetings as a child, this building with its exquisite cornices on the facade and the open interior had always sparked her imagination.

Pressing her face against the glass, she gasped at the transformation. The refinished oak floors gleamed. The crown moulding had been faithfully restored.

"Quite the project that was, I don't mind telling you."

Hand on her heart, she whirled. "Oh, Miss Helen. You startled me."

The diminutive, always well-put-together old woman stood at her elbow. She'd been so absorbed by the interior, Juliet hadn't heard her approach.

She nudged her chin at the pie plate the elderly woman clutched. "Who's that for, Miss Helen?"

"Dottie Walker's granddaughter had a baby. I'm on my way there."

Another sweet feature of small-town life. Southern women could be counted on through births, deaths and everything in between to make sure no one went hungry.

Helen motioned to the window. "Sign went up yesterday."

"The society did a beautiful job restoring this project." Juliet turned to the store. "The light is amazing."

Helen smiled at their reflections. "Good bones."

"Like you."

"And your gentle-hearted mother." Helen patted her arm. "Apples never fall far from the tree, my dear. The society is extremely motivated with this one. The lease is rent to own. Available to local entrepreneurs for an extremely low rate."

Juliet cocked her head.

The older woman smiled. "My grandson is the listing agent."

"You're not suggesting I consider leasing the old Whitaker building for Paw Pals, are you, Miss Helen?"

The old woman raised a thin, plucked eyebrow. "Why not? This architectural gem deserves to be occupied by someone with an appreciation for its beauty. I know you've always had a special feeling for this place."

"My life is in Greensboro, Miss Helen. My business, if I get the grant—"

"You'll get the grant."

Juliet crossed her arms. "But the hospital is in Greensboro."

"Did I misunderstand that the entire basis of your proposal was for a therapy dog nonprofit to serve underserved rural areas?"

"No, ma'am, you did not misunderstand."

Helen pursed her wrinkled lips. "Then perhaps it would make sense to establish your headquarters in Laurel Grove. An underserved rural area." Her powdered cheeks lifted. "And we'd all love to have you live closer. Food for thought at least, right?"

"Yes, ma'am."

"Location, location, location." Helen sniffed. "Have you forgotten about the parking lot in the back? Not many downtown properties can offer free parking for customers and employees. Won't take much for a forward-thinking businessperson to see the potential of this investment and snatch it up."

Miss Helen wasn't wrong. Even with the grant, comparable real estate property in Greensboro might be beyond her reach. Juliet took another look at the polished floors. Something about this property had always tugged at her heart.

"Don't I look a fright." Helen frowned at herself in the glass. "Like something the cat dragged down the street."

"You look your usual, lovely self, Miss Helen, and you know it." She hugged the old woman. A faint scent of lavender wafted past her nose. "You're walking to Dottie Walker's place?" She frowned.

Last year, Helen's driving license had been gently but firmly revoked after a series of unfortunate encounters with a dozen or so mailboxes.

The temperature in late May was a breeze compared to what July's humidity would bring when North Carolina became—for all intents and purposes—an outdoor sauna. But Helen lived on one side of Laurel Grove, not far from Juliet's childhood home in one of the older sections. Dottie Walker lived clear on the other side in one of the newer—circa 1950s—neighborhoods.

"Miss Helen, could I drop you off at Miss Dottie's house?"

The older woman put her hand to her pearls. "Well, that would be right kind of you, dear. But I don't want to take you out of your way."

"No trouble at all." Juliet took her arm. "We don't want the pie melting before you give it to the new mom."

Juliet had just dropped off Helen when she received an urgent text from her mother. Doctor called with results. Please come ASAP.

She read the message three times, trying to decipher if it was good news or bad. Palming the wheel, she returned to the knit shop.

Ringing up a customer, her mother motioned to the sitting area. Juliet waited with barely concealed impatience. But soon enough, the customer exited. For once, they had the store to themselves.

"Mom?" She swallowed. "What did the doctor say?"

Her mother sank onto the sofa beside her. "Dr. Woodbridge called the abnormal cells 'carcinoma in situ.'" Her mom flipped through a small pad of paper. "I wrote down everything she said so I'd remember to tell you."

She squeezed her mother's hand. "We're going to tackle this together. We'll—"

"Despite the scary-sounding name, Dr. Woodbridge wanted to make sure I understood the biopsy indicated precancer."

Juliet stared at her. "Precancer?"

"The cells, the changes in the tissue, were low-grade." Her mom pushed her glasses higher on the bridge of her nose. "Low-grade changes are unlikely to become cervical cancer."

Juliet's mouth trembled. "You *don't* have cancer?"

Her mother's eyes shone. "The doctor will keep a close watch to make sure my situation doesn't change, but it's good news."

"The best news."

She threw her arms around her mom. "Thank you, God."

"Amen." Her mother gave her a watery smile. "The doctor has scheduled a follow-up appointment for me in a few weeks, but I feel I've been given a second chance at life. And I don't mean to waste it."

Out of sheer relief, for several moments they shed a few tears together. But the bell jangled and another customer swooped in with a knitting crisis. Her mother's phone also started blowing up with texts from the Knit-Knackers looking for an update.

Juliet shook her head. "How did they know?"

She and her mom looked at each other.

"Laurel Grove grapevine," they said simultaneously and laughed so hysterically the knitter shot them a faintly alarmed glance.

Juliet left her mother to detangle the knitting disaster. She could think of only one person she wanted to share the good news with—a certain incredibly easy-on-the-eyes police detective.

On the way, she retrieved Moose. At Rob's, Sophie ran down the steps toward them. After that, there was the usual lovefest between the little girl and the tiny dog.

Following at a slower pace, Rob smiled, and her heart did that becoming predictable dance inside her chest.

Slightly breathless, she shared her mom's good news.

"I'm so thrilled for both of you." He gave her a measured glance. "Would it violate your professional code of conduct if I hugged you?"

She gave him a long, slow look from the corner of her eye. "With the case file closed, I see no conflicts."

His arms went around her. Being with him felt so right. So safe. So good...

Too good? She frowned. Now that Sophie was doing well and her mom's results were in, there was no longer any reason to delay her departure.

But for the first time, she didn't relish returning to her lonely condo. It felt nicer here. Happier. Better.

What would it hurt to spend a few more days in Laurel Grove? There was no harm in staying over the weekend. It wasn't like she'd heard from the hospital board yet about Paw Pals. There was nothing in Greensboro awaiting her return.

The weekend turned into Monday. Monday into Tuesday. She continued to make excuses to herself for not packing up Moose and taking her leave of the Melbournes. Yet always at the back of her mind, like a dark thundercloud on the horizon, lay the inevitable reckoning.

At this rate, she might never leave. An idea that scared her. But not enough to say goodbye.

As the days continued to unfold and Juliet remained in Laurel Grove, Rob went from cautiously optimistic to increasing confidence he might convince her to stay.

When he and Uncle Adrian went on an early-morning doughnut run to the new bakery, Rob shared his doubts about returning to the Greensboro PD. "What do you think?"

Adrian examined the pastry case. "I think the chocolate-covered custard is calling my name."

"You know what I mean."

Adrian placed his order along with Rob's and they waited.

"I think… I think the evidence suggests doughnuts are not just a law enforcement stereotype." Adrian smirked.

Rob gave him a look.

"I also think you need to have a conversation with your neighbor about your interest in exploring local, vocational opportunities."

"Vernon Stancil?"

"The very one." Adrian accepted the white bag from the girl on the other side of the counter. "He may have retired from barbering, but he's still the town mayor."

Rob tried to pay for their orders, but as usual, the down-to-earth farmer would have none of it.

They ambled out of the shop to his uncle's truck.

Adrian climbed into the cab. "Indications from the Laurel Grove grapevine suggest there's something coming available that may not be so much a change as an upgrade. Perfect for your wheelhouse of skills."

"The grapevine?" Rob slid into the passenger seat. "You guys are worse than the women."

"Vernon will have good advice for you. Let him know you're interested in working in Laurel Grove."

Rob tilted his head. "You think Vernon might know of something?"

His uncle cranked the engine. "I do."

"I'll talk to him then."

Pulling onto Main, his uncle steered toward Rob's house. "How's things with the fair Juliet?"

Rob grinned. "Sweeter than these doughnuts."

"Happy to hear it." The older man chuckled. "Now try not to mess things up. She's a keeper."

"Yes, sir." He settled his shoulders against the seat. "If I can convince her to have me."

Later that morning, Sophie informed him and Juliet she wanted to be a therapy dog handler when she grew up. "Like you, Miss Juliet. How did you do it?"

"I'll show you." Juliet kissed Sophie's head.

Every time she did that, he got visions of the two of them putting Sophie to bed every night. Playing with her. Praying with her. His child becoming their child.

"Whether Moose is at school being the class reading dog or visiting people at the hospital, his main job is to make them smile."

Sophie grinned. "Like he makes me smile."

Juliet pulled the purple vest out of the backpack and put it on him. Rob realized he hadn't seen Moose wearing it in over a week. Probably not since Mrs. Larsen gave Sophie the all clear.

So Juliet had been hanging out with them because she wanted to be with them. Not because she was working with them.

"Moose went through a lot of training to get his AKC Canine Good Citizen certificate and then more training before finally taking the Therapy Dogs International test."

Sophie's eyes widened. "What did Moose have to do?"

Juliet clipped the leash on Moose. "The testers had a clipboard. They were checking his temperament. His obedience to commands. His ability to be with children and cope around wheelchairs."

She put Moose through his paces. Sitting. Lying down. Staying. "We practice when we're not on a case so Moose doesn't forget. He knows when the purple vest goes on, it's time to work."

Juliet walked Moose around the perimeter of the living room. "The test evaluator touched Moose's ears and tail to make sure he wasn't sensitive to a stranger's touch."

She dropped a heavy book on the hardwood. Sophie covered her ears, but Moose didn't move a muscle. Opening his jaws wide, he actually yawned.

Rob laughed.

"They dropped bedpans to make sure he wasn't easily startled by loud noises." Tearing off part of a leftover doughnut, Juliet dropped the piece on the floor and walked Moose right by it.

The little dog didn't give it a second glance.

"Moose, I salute you." Rocking on his heels, Rob folded his arms across his chest. "Not sure I could do that."

Juliet's mouth curved. "I know you couldn't."

Sophie bounced from her seat on the sofa. "What else did Moose have to do?"

"Moose practiced meeting people at an assisted-living facility near my condo. He had to show the evaluator he was a good, patient listener."

Sophie nodded, her small braids bobbing. "Moose is a very good listener."

"And, of course, Moose had to demonstrate how well he got along with other dogs."

"But we don't have another dog here." Sophie's face brightened. "I know. Daddy can pretend to be a dog."

Rob cut his gaze to Juliet. "Uh, what?"

Juliet's eyes twinkled. "Great idea."

Rob got down on the floor. "Taking one for the team, guys."

His physical therapist had released him from further therapy. The leg was no longer sore, only a little stiff when rain was forecast.

"What kind of dog should I be, Soph?"

"The kind that barks."

He and Juliet laughed.

"I think I can manage that." He let loose a yowl that sounded part coyote.

Juliet rolled her eyes. "Such an overachiever."

He winked at her because he enjoyed seeing the soft, pink blush suffuse her cheeks. "Takes one to know one."

"If you *were* a dog…" Hands on her hips, she scrutinized him until he passed his hand over his head, imagining he still had bed hair. "You'd be a Siberian husky."

His brows rose. "I would?"

"They have such gorgeous blue eyes."

"Ah." He grinned. "Do you have a personal preference for blue eyes, Juliet?"

"I might." She blushed prettily again. "But don't let it go to that overlarge head of yours."

Bored with grown-up talk, Sophie put Moose through his paces. After lunch, Juliet offered to run Sophie to the Ewe. Lesley had invited his daughter to help her with a craft—a collage of Moose's paw prints.

"Paint and a preschooler." Rob shuddered. "Better your mother than me."

"Mom loves working with children. Little girls in particular. They'll have a blast."

Holding Moose on a leash, Sophie was already out the door, eager for her craft date. He caught Juliet's hand.

Rob twined his fingers through hers. "If you come

back and hang out with Sophie's dear old dad, I promise to make it worth your while."

"Such an inflated opinion of yourself," she chided, but her mouth quirked.

He kissed her hand and was inordinately pleased when she flashed him a full-on smile.

"Okay... If you insist... You talked me into it."

His heart turned over. It hadn't taken him long to discover her secret power. He was putty in her hands. And he'd like nothing more than to spend the rest of his life like that.

Ten minutes later, she returned. He was waiting for her on the porch, but as she reached the bottom step, her phone dinged. Reading the text, her hand went to her throat.

Gut tightening, he rose. "Is something wrong?"

Her gaze lifted to his. "I got it," she whispered. "I got the grant."

Leaping forward, she threw her arms around his neck. Laughing, he caught her and twirled her around.

Their laughter slowly faded. He became conscious how good she felt in his arms. How right. How inevitable. Or so it seemed to him.

Breathing rapidly, they stared at each other for a long moment. He wanted to kiss her. But she was still so hung up on the loss of her husband. If this wondrous thing between them were to happen at all, he had to let her take the lead.

Much as it pained him, he let go of her and took a step back.

Juliet felt the loss of his arms around her like a physical blow. A harbinger of winter after the warmth of a Laurel Grove spring.

She took a step toward him, bridging the distance between them. "Kiss me, Rob."

A muscle ticked in his jaw. "You want me to kiss you?"

Sudden doubt assailed her. The awkward, geeky seventeen-year-old she'd been once upon a time reared inside her, threatening to overcome the confident, secure woman she'd become.

Just as she began to lose her nerve, he placed his hands on her shoulders. "Don't overanalyze what I said. I only wanted to be sure you were sure."

"I'm sure." She tilted her head. "Kiss me, please," she whispered.

Raising his hands, he cradled her face between his palms. He pulled her closer. She closed her eyes.

Lowering his head, he brushed his lips across hers. And stopped. Giving her the chance to pull away if she chose. But she didn't.

Joy pierced her heart.

She fit into his arms as if she'd been made for him. And he for her.

What she felt for him was so... So much more than she'd ever imagined herself feeling for anyone.

She wanted this—them—more than she wanted anything else in life. More than she wanted Josh?

Then, a thousand different memories of Josh cascaded through her mind. But one memory in particular flashed through her brain with a sharp, brittle clarity—Josh's funeral.

Juliet planted her hands against Rob's chest and pushed him away.

Startled, he dropped his hands. "What is it? What's wrong?"

"This is wrong."

He moved as if to touch her, but she shook him off. "I can't do this. Not again."

She wouldn't put herself in a position to ever feel that lost again. Had she learned nothing from what happened to her mother? Had she forgotten the pain of feeling like the only kid in Laurel Grove without a father?

What had she been thinking to kiss Rob? To lower the walls she'd placed around her heart.

Five years ago, she'd clutched the folded American flag against her black dress. And she'd wept during the mournful dirge of "Taps."

She mustn't ever forget—

"Juliet, I love you."

"No. Don't say that."

Juliet put her hand to her mouth. More than just a memory, his kiss lingered. Why had she kissed him? She couldn't stay in Laurel Grove. Not another minute.

Chapter Twelve

"I love you, Juliet."

As soon as the words left his mouth, Rob knew he'd made a big mistake. She wasn't ready to hear his feelings. Not yet. But the truth inside him could no longer be denied.

The truth he'd first begun to recognize the day she told him about her lost baby.

Eyes wide with panic, she stared at him. Something akin to dread lurked in their dark depths. "You can't love me."

"But I do." He reached for her, but she dodged his hand. If only she'd let him touch her, reassure her. "There's no use denying it."

She stood there frozen. Like a wary woodland creature, ready to bolt at the slightest provocation.

"Give us a chance. I won't pressure you. We can take this at whatever pace you say. We could be happy."

Juliet's expression twisted. "You don't understand, Rob. You have Sophie and your aunt and uncle. Josh lost his family young. He has no one but me."

"Had, Juliet," Rob growled. "Josh is dead."

She flinched as if he'd slapped her. "Don't you see? If I don't remember him, no one else will."

"If Josh Newkirk is half the man you say, I can't believe for one minute he'd want you to throw away your life on a memory." Rob widened his stance. "Not when you have so much life ahead of you and so much love to give. To Sophie. To me."

Her eyes glinted. "I never said I loved you."

Rob grabbed her hand. "But you do love me. You and I have experienced real love once before. We know what it looks like. What it feels like."

She shook her head so the long strands of her hair whipped her cheeks. "I won't love you. I… I can't love you." Her voice hitched. "Not if it means losing Josh. I can't do that to him. I'm returning to Greensboro tomorrow."

"Don't do this, Juliet. Don't shut me out." His desperation mounted, a coiled fist in his chest, tightening so hard he could scarcely breathe. "Don't sentence yourself to loneliness. You deserve more than that. Josh would want you to have more than that. Don't throw away the love Sophie and I have for you."

Her mouth flattened. "It's not fair to bring Sophie into it."

Rob didn't care about being fair. He was growing ever more frantic at the prospect of losing her completely.

He backed away a step. "We don't have to rush things. We can take things slow." His heart jackhammered. "Just don't walk out of our lives."

She wrapped her arms around herself. "I think a clean break is best."

"Best for who?" He laughed, the sound without mirth. "Not for me. Not for Sophie. And although you're too stubborn to see it, least of all for you."

"You're wrong." She jutted her jaw. "I have a life, a good fulfilling life, in Greensboro."

"A life consumed with mourning a dead man. That's no life, Juliet." He raked his hand through his hair. "I don't think that's even the real reason you're in such a panic to leave. I think you're scared. Terrified of letting go of safe, comfortable, dead Josh—"

"Stop it!" she rasped.

"Because once you do, you'll have to face how lonely you are and how much you need someone. And that frightens you more than losing this perfect version of Josh, the man you've put on a pedestal."

She sucked in a breath. "You are the most arrogant, insufferable…"

"You're terrified to love anyone who might fail you, or let you down, or leave you."

"Josh left me," she wailed. "Just like my father."

Rob wanted nothing more than to spend his life loving away her pain. But she wouldn't let him. Why wouldn't she let him?

"Josh didn't leave you on purpose, Juliet." Rob gentled his voice. "He died."

She squeezed her eyes closed. "I know that."

"Do you? Loving means losing to you. It's gotten all mixed-up in your head. I'm not like your father. I'd never leave you, Juliet."

"You wouldn't mean to." Her eyes flew open and the sadness in them stole his breath. "Josh didn't mean to, either. I made him promise that I'd be the one to die first. Because I couldn't bear to be left behind." She gritted her teeth. "But he broke his promise. He left me."

Rob ached to take her in his arms. "No one can make a promise like that. Our lives are in God's hands. Not our own. Is this about my job?" He hunched his shoulders. "Because we can work through that. We can work through anything as long as we're together."

"You weren't on the job when you were shot. You could go out to the store for a birthday gift—" she threw out her hands "—and never come home again."

"So what's your plan, Juliet? To never care about anyone ever again? To never allow anyone else to care about you?" He shook his head. "That's no life. In the end, your cocoon becomes a tomb."

She put her hands over her ears, reminding him of Sophie. "You're wrong."

He tugged at her hands. "Sure, life is sometimes painful. Life is sometimes hard. But it's also wonderful and beautiful and so much more."

Juliet made a motion as if to move past him.

"Stand there and tell me to my face you don't love me."

Her chin wobbled. "I... I can't."

Rob reached for her. "Jules..."

She pushed his hand away. "I can't tell you I love you."

He tightened his jaw. "You mean you *won't*. This isn't about Josh and you know it. This is about you and me and Sophie. And the life we could have together."

Juliet crossed her arms in front of her as if she were cold. "There is no life for us."

"Some people never get one chance at true love. We've been given a second chance."

Did she want him to beg her? He would. If that's what it took to get her to stay. What could he do to break through to her? To get her to listen.

"Please don't do this, Juliet. Let yourself be happy. Why won't you give us a chance?"

"The why doesn't matter. My reasons are as impossible to unravel as a knotted skein of yarn." She turned her face toward the street. "Please tell Sophie goodbye for me."

"Tell her yourself." He folded his arms. "I'm not going to make it easy for you to break her heart the way you're breaking mine. I love you, Juliet. I love you."

"I'm not ready to say those words to you. I'll probably never be able to say those words to anyone ever again." Her lovely brown eyes swam with tears. "I have nothing to offer you, Rob."

He shook his head, angry at her stubborn refusal to allow him to love her. "You have yourself. And that is so much more than you realize, than you can possibly understand. You are everything to me and to Sophie. I will never forget the weeks we've shared. I couldn't if I wanted to, and I don't want to." He scrubbed his forehead with his hand. "Though perhaps you find us—me—more easily forgettable."

"That's not true." Her face became stricken. "I never meant to hurt you or Sophie."

He looked at her, his heart in his eyes. "Juliet…"

"Don't." Taking a deep breath, she turned from him. "I… I'm sorry, Rob." Squaring her shoulders, she headed toward her car.

And like the idiot he was for giving her the power to destroy his life and his child's, he watched her drive away.

Knees buckling, he sat down abruptly on the top step, his dreams for the future burned to ashes around him. He dropped his head into his hands.

She was sorry?

He was the one who was sorry. Sorry for the bleakness of the life she was willing to consign herself. Sorry for the mother Sophie would never have.

But most of all, he was sorry for what they'd never be together.

* * *

That night, her mom was ecstatic at the news about the grant, but less thrilled by her imminent departure.

Behind her eyeglasses, her mother's dark eyes sharpened. "Does Rob know?"

"I told him this afternoon."

Avoiding the questions in her gaze, Juliet made a lame excuse about needing to pack and fled to her bedroom.

Juliet scanned the room for any more of her belongings. Seeing none, she shut the suitcase with a firm click. And became equally firm in turning her thoughts from Rob's words.

Sophie proved more difficult to banish. The little girl had made so many strides toward becoming the happy, bubbly child she'd been before the shooting.

Juliet couldn't bear it if her absence caused a setback to Sophie's recovery.

Sinking onto the mattress, Juliet heard Moose's nails clicking across the hardwood floor, keeping her mom company in the kitchen.

Who would keep Sophie company after Juliet left? Or for that matter, Rob?

She mustn't think of him. Or of how lonely he'd seemed when they first met. How he and Sophie had opened up to her. First with friendship. Followed by love.

Did she love Rob?

She pillowed her head in her hands. This couldn't be happening to her. She'd never asked to experience these feelings for him.

She didn't—mustn't—couldn't… She gritted her teeth. She wouldn't allow herself to love Rob.

But what about Sophie?

Tears pricked her eyelids. The idea of the little girl's

sadness tore at her. She loved Sophie with all her heart. She could at least admit to that.

"What should I do about Sophie, God?" she whispered. "But please don't tell me this means I have to stay in Laurel Grove."

Like a drowning woman, she clung to the image she carried in her mind of Josh's eyes. His laugh. But lately, she could no longer hear his voice in her head.

The things she'd loved about him were slowly but surely being eroded by Rob's bright blue eyes. Rob's laugh. His voice. The memory of the life she'd had with Josh was slipping out of her grasp.

"I can't stay here. I just can't." Ending on a slight wail, she clamped her hand over her mouth.

Her eyes darted toward the closed door, horrified her mom might have heard her.

She had no business telling God what to do in one breath and then asking for help in the next, but her feelings were all over the place.

"Please show me, God," she rasped.

And then, an almost unthinkable solution came to mind. It was not at all what she'd expected. Stunned, she lay back on the duvet.

God might not ask her to stay in Laurel Grove, but He couldn't really be asking her to do this instead, could He?

Her stomach knotted. She wrestled with herself until her mom knocked on the door to call her to dinner.

Composing herself, she ventured into the kitchen. Moose pattered over with a flurry of enthusiastic barks. As if they'd been separated weeks instead of minutes, his tail flicked rapidly.

Moose's delight stabbed her heart. She lavished some love on him before sliding into her chair and setting him on the floor beside her feet.

Her mom said a blessing over the meal. But Juliet picked at the food on her plate.

"I take it that telling Rob you were leaving didn't go well."

A wrenching dismay filled her at the memory of their parting. "It was awful." Juliet sighed. "He told me he loved me."

Her mom gave her a mock frown. "What a terrible thing to say to someone. I'm shocked."

"Mom. I'm being serious."

"So am I. It's as obvious as the nose on your face how he feels about you. And how you feel about him."

"I don't—" She pressed her lips together. "I'm not going to discuss Rob with you."

"How did Sophie react?"

Juliet laid down her fork. "She was with you. I didn't tell her."

Her mother frowned. "You're not going to leave that child without saying goodbye, are you?"

"No." Juliet swallowed. "I wouldn't do that to her. Besides, she's become very attached to Moose."

Her mother laid her hand on Juliet's. "Not only Moose."

"I can't stand to leave her hurting. Moose has a bond with her like he's never had with anyone but me. I've had this idea…" She swallowed. "I was thinking about leaving Moose with Sophie."

"For how long?"

Juliet's mouth wobbled. "Forever."

Her mother sat back. "Are you sure you want to do this? After everything Moose has meant to you."

"I love Moose dearly, but what I feel for Sophie…" Juliet swiped at her eyes. "I love her like I would've loved my child."

"She could be your child, Juliet." Her mom's eyes glistened. "If you can open your heart to her, why is it so hard to open your heart to her father?"

"Rob said I was afraid to leave the safety of my cocoon."

"Is he right?"

"Probably." Her eyes flitted away from her mother's penetrating gaze. "But telling yourself to stop being afraid doesn't actually mean you stop being afraid." Her shoulders slumped. "That sounds ridiculous when I say it out loud, doesn't it?"

"Putting a name to the fear is the first step, but fear doesn't go away overnight." Her mother blew out a breath. "Are you sure you want to make such an incredible sacrifice?"

"As sure as I've ever been of anything." She raised her hands. "I can't be here for Sophie, but Moose can love her for me."

"What about when you get back to your condo? You'll be so alone."

Exactly why she'd adopted Moose in the first place.

"Maybe it's time to face the fear. To confront the loneliness."

Her mother cocked her head. "What about Paw Pals and your work at the hospital?"

She gave her mom a tentative smile. "Receiving the grant means I'll finally be able to get a real office. To train and hire other dog handlers to continue the work. The mission of Paw Pals will continue." Her smile slipped a notch. "Just not with me on the front lines. At least for a while."

Rising, her mom hugged her. "I'm so proud of the brave, caring woman you've become, darling."

Juliet knew she was anything but brave. A brave person would let herself love Rob.

Returning her mother's hug, for a moment, she wished she could once again be a little girl. When her mother's embrace solved all of life's ills.

Breathing in her mom's rosewater scent one final time, she let go of her mother.

"I won't stay away as long next time, Mom. I promise. We've got your follow-up at the doctor's in a few weeks."

Her mother touched her cheek. "Rob is nothing like your father, Juliet."

She jerked. "I know that."

"Do you? Truly?"

Juliet bit her lip, hesitant to voice a thought she'd never had the courage to ask out loud. Something she'd wondered ever since she was old enough to notice everyone else had a father, except for her.

"Mom, do you ever regret…" She choked.

Her mother's eyes widened. "Regret having you? Never."

"But if you'd known that after he found out you were pregnant with me, he'd walk away…"

"I would've wanted you just the same." Her mother raised Juliet's chin. "He was the mistake, my darling. Never you."

For a moment, they cried together.

"I'm sorry his inability to love you as you deserved has meant you've lived your life alone." She peered into her mom's face. "I promise to do better about staying in touch."

Her mother's health scare had been a wake-up call. Life was precious and so very short. Evelyn had been right that first day. She only had one mom. And she meant to cherish every moment for as long as the Lord allowed.

"Don't count my love life a lost cause too soon." Her mom tossed her an irrepressible grin. "Watch out, Laurel Grove. This old girl isn't ready for the pasture yet. Not by a long shot."

Later, Juliet texted Rob to ask if she could drop by to say goodbye to Sophie the next morning.

An hour ticked by with no response. Her head pounded. Her heart thudded. He must be so terribly angry with her. And she didn't blame him.

Just when she'd begun to despair, he responded with just the one word, Yes.

She ought to let him know about Moose so he'd have time to prepare. She touched the tip of her finger to the screen to type the message and then pulled back. The blinking cursor mocked her.

Perhaps it was better to ask him in person rather than through an impersonal text. She hoped he'd see the wisdom of her decision. Sophie's well-being was all that mattered.

Juliet spent the rest of the long evening second-guessing herself. How could she bear to return to her empty condo without her dearest companion?

Sensing her strange mood, Moose glued himself to her. And she loved on the best little dog in the world through her tears.

Chapter Thirteen

The next morning, she and her mom left the house at the same time.

"Let me know when you reach your condo so I'll know you arrived safely." Waving, her mom headed downtown.

Her car packed and Moose strapped in, Juliet drove toward Rob's neighborhood. She hadn't slept much last night. She hadn't been able to eat breakfast, either.

The lack of sleep and food was catching up with her. She felt light-headed and her stomach felt like a corkscrew.

In the driveway, she sat for a moment with her hands resting on the wheel. Taking one last look at the house that could have become her home. If she were braver.

She would have decorated the broad front porch with urns of crimson red geraniums. Maybe adding vibrant, color-splashed cushions on the wicker furniture, inviting friends to sit a spell and visit.

It was far easier to contemplate the house than the people she was leaving behind. The family she was running from. The life she was choosing never to live.

Moose barked, a short yip, to remind her she wasn't alone.

Her eyes darted to the rearview mirror. "You're right, Moose. I'd best do this before I lose my nerve."

Leaving the windows down for airflow, she got out of the car. Bracing her shoulders, eyes on the path, she moved toward the porch. Rob came out of the house.

She stutter-stepped to a halt. Her hand went to her throat.

"Juliet," he rasped in that early-morning, before-coffee voice of his.

His seen-better-days gray T-shirt hung untucked from his jeans. With dark shadows beneath his eyes, he looked as bad as she felt. But even on a bad day, he looked amazingly good. Too good for her peace of mind.

On leave from the Greensboro PD, his beard stubble had grown over the last few weeks, giving him a slightly rakish, infinitely appealing look.

She knotted her hands together. "Where's Sophie?"

Hands jammed in his pockets, he nudged his head toward the house. "In the backyard with Aunt Evie. I didn't tell her you were coming. I didn't want her to get her hopes up in case…"

She reddened. "In case I didn't show?"

"In case this morning didn't work out." He angled. "I'll take you—"

"Wait." She grabbed his arm.

As soon as she touched him, she realized her mistake. She dropped her hand as if stung. He must have felt it, too. But his only reaction was to turn away.

Already he was distancing himself from her. It was to be expected. But she hadn't anticipated the widening gulf between them hurting so much.

She gulped. "I'm glad we have this chance to talk before I see Sophie."

A quick light sprang into his eyes. "You've changed your mind about leaving?"

"No…" She felt lower than a worm, watching the hope fade from his face.

He hunched his shoulders. "What then? I imagine we've said everything we can to each other. I'm sure you're anxious to put Laurel Grove in your rearview." His handsome mouth twisted. "The sooner, the better."

She'd hurt him. Badly. And she had no one to blame but herself.

"I'm sorry." His Adam's apple bobbed. "I didn't mean that the way it came out."

He raked his hand over his head, leaving the short ends standing on edge. He stood there, looking strangely vulnerable and young.

She had an insane urge to run her hand over his hair. To soothe and comfort him.

Lest she give in to the impulse, she curled her fingers into a fist and clamped it against her thigh. "I need to get Moose out of the car, but first I wanted to ask you a favor."

A muscle ticked in his jaw. His gaze locked onto hers. She flushed. Well aware she was the last person on earth who ought to be asking him for favors.

He folded his arms across his chest. "What is it you want, Juliet?"

You.

She sucked in a breath at the treacherous thought. No, that wasn't it at all. She didn't want the complication of Rob in her life. That's why she was going to Greensboro. Why she couldn't stay.

Could she?

"If it's a reference, sure…" He shrugged. "A review. A testimonial. Whatever you need for Paw Pals."

She could feel her body starting to shake. Her heart betraying what her head knew to be unalterably true. "I… I'd like you to adopt Moose for Sophie's sake."

His eyes widened. And she could tell that of all the things he might have imagined she'd ask him, this hadn't made the list.

"You want to give Moose to Sophie?"

She nodded.

He cocked his head. "Why would you do that?"

Despite the sultry morning, she wrapped her arms around herself. "Because Sophie needs Moose more than I do. Somehow Moose understands that."

"But Moose is your dog." Rob shook his head. "He won't be happy without you."

"I spent all night thinking about this. A dog picks his person. At the rescue shelter, he picked me. But now, I think he's picked Sophie for the next season of his life."

A breeze played with a loose tendril of her hair. She tucked the errant strand behind her ear. Rob's gaze followed the motion of her hand.

The longing on his face gutted her. Playing havoc with her determination to leave Laurel Grove. To walk away from him.

Her heart squeezing, she clung to the threads of her resolve. "Moose loves her. I've never seen him bond with anyone so much. I believe this is the right thing for both of them."

Rob's forehead scrunched. "I don't know about this, Juliet."

"I realize taking on the care of a dog only adds to your responsibilities as a single dad."

He speared her with a lightning flash of blue. "It's not that. I'm thinking this is a rash decision—" again, his eyes cut to her "—you'll come to regret. What about Paw Pals? How can you do your thing without your dog?"

"I'll be much too busy interviewing and training people to do hospital visits myself." She shrugged, trying for a nonchalance she wasn't close to feeling. "Eventually, I'll get around to finding another dog."

"We're that easily replaced in your life, are we?"

She glared at him. "That's not what I meant."

"All of us, except Josh." Rob leaned heavily against the railing. "The last thing I wanted to do was replace him. I could no more replace what he meant in your life than you could replace what Katrina meant to mine. I only wanted a chance to carve out my own place in your heart, not take his."

She blinked furiously at him. Her throat felt raw from the effort to not bawl in front of him.

"Moose can't take the place of you, Juliet. A dog isn't going to stop Sophie—stop us—from missing you."

"Children are resilient. She'll be fine. With time, the pain of parting—like the trauma that led to our meeting—will pass."

He straightened. "If you're sure this is what you want, we'd be thrilled to share our home with Moose." He scratched his head. "And Fluff-Fluff, too?"

It didn't quite reach his eyes, but he did his best to smile. A crooked smile. The weaker version of his famously knee-buckling smile. But still possessing enough of its usual potency to gobsmack her senses.

Nobody this irresistibly charming ought to be allowed to roam unsupervised among a defenseless public. Not without PSAs. Or Kevlar.

"Fluff-Fluff, too," she whispered when the world stopped whirling.

He climbed the steps and held the door for her. "We

should talk to Sophie before we bring Moose into the picture."

She entered the house. "Good idea. All rational thought tends to flee once Moose is on the scene."

He followed her inside, letting the door close behind him. "Same thing happens to me with you." He walked past her to the back of the house.

She was left staring, dumbfounded, after his broad shoulders. Gobsmacked all over again.

He waited for her to catch up. His lips twitched. She wasn't sure what, but something seemed to amuse him mightily.

She stepped onto the porch. "You don't fight fair."

"All's fair in love and war, Juliet."

Her heart thundered at the expression on his face. "And what is this?" She gestured between them.

"I'll leave that for you to choose. But you need to know I'm not easily deterred. Like a dog with a bone, I don't give up."

Juliet frowned. He'd been angry and hurt just moments earlier. Now he appeared calmer, lighter, determined...

Outside, he cupped his hand around his mouth. "Sophie! Look who's here to see you," he called.

There was no time to ponder his whiplash mood swing. At the jungle gym with Evelyn, Sophie's head snapped up.

"Miss Juliet!" the little girl cried. "You came back." She rushed across the lawn.

Flinging her arms around Juliet's waist, Sophie engulfed her in a tight hug. She buried her face in Juliet's blue shirt.

Juliet inhaled the sweet, little girl fragrance of her. Shampoo. Fresh air. And the sprig of lilac Evelyn had surely tucked into the headband on the crown of her silky hair.

The older woman ambled past. "I'm going to leave you to your reunion. Suddenly, I find myself so parched…" She disappeared inside the house.

"You came back. You came back," Sophie mumbled into her shirt.

Juliet threw him a worried glance.

Rob squatted beside his daughter. "Sophie, we talked about this last night. Juliet is moving back to her home in Greensboro."

Her gut constricted. The condo wasn't her home. It was her retreat from the world.

A haven from pain. Her safety net. But never home. Her gaze cut around the oak-lined perimeter of the yard. Not like here.

Sophie loosened her tight grip. Already she missed Sophie's warmth.

"But she came back," Sophie repeated, in case they'd been too slow to catch it the first time.

A sinking feeling cramped her stomach. Because he was just that kind of man, Rob came to her rescue. Always a hero. Her hero.

"Juliet came to say goodbye, Soph."

Sophie's eyebrows like tiny twin caterpillars bunched. "But I don't want to say goodbye."

"I don't either, Sophie. But sometimes we have to say goodbye." He scrubbed his face. "Whether we want to or not. Whether we're ready to or not."

The child wrapped her arms around her dad. "Like when my mommy died?"

A spasm of pain crisscrossed his face. Gone so quickly as to almost be imagined.

"Yes." His voice became hoarse. "Exactly like that."

Capturing his face between the palms of her hands,

Sophie pressed her forehead against his. "I'm not a baby anymore, Daddy."

"No, you're not. Which is why…" He lifted her into his arms. "Juliet also came by to give you a special gift."

Sophie's head jerked toward Juliet. "A gift for me?" She clasped her hands under her chin. "What is it?"

He kissed her cheek. "A big girl gift. Juliet wants Moose to live with us. Would you like Moose to be your dog?"

Sophie's mouth dropped. "For my very own?" She twisted toward Juliet. "In my house? With me? And Daddy? Fluff-Fluff, too?"

"Yes." Juliet rolled her eyes at Rob's grin. "Fluff-Fluff, too."

Sophie shrieked, startling them both. She squirmed to get down from his arms.

The screened door screeched.

Evelyn poked her head out. "Everything okay out here?"

"Peachy." He set his daughter on the ground and clamped his hand to his ear. "Despite a probable hearing loss." He shook his head as if to ring the noise from his ears.

"Aunt Evie!" Sophie danced. "Moose is going to be my dog."

Evelyn smiled. "Glad to hear it." Fluttering her hand, she went inside again.

He looked at Juliet. "Was it just me, or did Aunt Evie look decidedly not surprised?"

She sighed. "The Knit-Knack grapevine strikes again."

He stuck his hands in his pockets. "There's a lot to love about Laurel Grove."

Yes. She looked at him. Yes, there was.

"We're going to go for walks. We'll do story time at

school. We'll have tea parties…" Sophie was practically doing handstands in the grass. "I have a dog. I have a dog. I Have A Dog!" she shouted.

He chuckled. "Just in case the rest of Laurel Grove hasn't heard yet."

"From the first day we met, this is what I prayed for her." Tears formed in Juliet's eyes. "For this happy, wonderful little girl to find her joy again."

"Thanks to you," he murmured.

She swiped a finger under her eye. "And Moose."

"Mostly you. Sophie! Come over here." He beckoned. "Juliet needs to go over Moose's routine with you before she gets on the road."

She blinked stupidly at him for a half second. This visit was supposed to be goodbye. But she'd gotten caught up with this man and his child. In the excitement. The hope. But he was right. It was time she was on her way to her real life.

A few weeks of bliss didn't constitute a life. At least, not her life.

She went over the basic information about caring for Moose. "I've printed everything out for you. It's in Moose's bag in the car."

Rob nodded. "I guess we should transfer his stuff into the house."

"And get Moose," Sophie said.

It took the three of them to bring everything inside. Sophie was beside herself placing Moose's doggie bed beside her own bed.

Then there was nothing left to do, except to say goodbye. Sophie cried. Moose whimpered. Juliet clung to them both.

"Aunt Evie!" Rob called into the house. "Would you bring Sophie and Moose into the kitchen with you?"

The door creaked open. Evelyn's big blue eyes—so like her nephew's—darted between them. Taking Sophie's hand and holding Moose's leash, the older lady led them into the house.

Eyes narrowed, head tilted, Rob peered at Juliet. As if working out a puzzle. About her.

Would he try to convince her to stay? She wasn't sure how much longer she could hold back the helpless, hopeless flood of emotion within her.

She choked back a sob. "I… I'm no good at goodbyes."

"Me neither, Juliet." His voice became brisk. "But life stands still for no one."

Without another word, he turned on his heel and disappeared inside the house. Shutting the door with a solid click.

She stared at the closed door. Was that it? This was goodbye? Pain exploded in her chest. Searing her heart.

But he was right. Life didn't stand still. He'd go on with his life. Which was entirely as it should be.

He'd meet someone. The new teacher at the school? The cute pharmacist, who'd transferred to the Laurel Grove store? Or perhaps the gorgeous veterinarian.

The notion left her feeling hollow.

No doubt her mom would keep her informed on the progress of his love life. He was too much of a catch to remain single forever. Any woman would be blessed to have him in her life.

Just not Juliet.

She cried all the way back to Greensboro.

Time did not always heal wounds.

Following Josh's death, a fact Juliet learned the hard way. If she'd imagined her feelings for Rob would fade, the next few weeks proved her wrong.

Spring drifted into summer. But despite her best efforts, the ache in her heart for Rob and Sophie failed to go away. If anything, her feelings only intensified.

In the waiting room at the doctor's office, she shifted in the chair. Her mom would be finished with her follow-up visit soon.

She talked to her mom every day and made it a point to get together in person at least once a week. Thus far, her mom had been understanding about meeting in Greensboro. Juliet hadn't yet found the courage to return to Laurel Grove.

There were too many reminders of Rob and Sophie there. And every chance she might accidentally run into them. Not something she was brave enough to face yet.

Her mother emerged from the inner office. Heart in her throat, Juliet rose. "What did the doctor say?"

"She wants to monitor me every six months." Her mom smiled. "But currently, the test results indicate I'm cancer-free."

Juliet threw her arms around her mother. "Thank You, Lord," she whispered.

Her mom gave her a quick squeeze. "The doctor's office makes me hungry. Let's do lunch."

"Absolutely. We need to celebrate your good news."

"Nothing fancy." Her mother wagged her finger. "I'm in the mood for comfort food."

"How about Yum Yum's?" She reached for her keys. "It's early enough to beat the corporate crowd."

"Sounds perfect." Her mom settled her purse strap on her shoulder. "And a beautiful day to sit outside at the picnic tables."

Juliet drove them across town toward the locally famous, hundred-year-old-plus restaurant noted for their hot dogs and milkshakes.

Under the shade of the enormous spreading branches of an oak tree, they sat on the wooden benches with their food.

Her mother took a bite of her hot dog and groaned with pleasure.

Juliet sipped her milkshake. "I'm guessing you're enjoying your lunch."

She cut her eyes at Juliet. "The best things in life are absolutely worth the wait."

Juliet's gaze tangled with her mom's. Sensing her mother was no longer referring to hot dogs, she flushed.

Her mom fingered a crinkle-cut fry. "You've been busy since you returned to Greensboro."

She welcomed the change in topic. She'd thrown herself into expanding Paw Pals. "I've had a lot of meetings with the grant committee."

"Have you finished hiring your team?"

She nodded. "About a dozen qualified dog therapy handlers."

Her mother's eyebrow rose. "Wow."

"Each one is vital to implementing the pilot programs I want to establish outside the hospital. At an assisted-living facility and a local elementary school."

"Your dream is coming true." Her mom covered Juliet's hand with her own. "I'm so happy for you. And proud. Have you found an office space?"

Juliet shook her head. "The hospital let me use a conference room to conduct the interviews."

Nothing had grabbed her imagination the way the old Whitaker building had in Laurel Grove. Ridiculous, of course.

Juliet's life was in Greensboro. Although, many of her staff already lived outside the city. The occasional meeting in Laurel Grove wouldn't have proven a hardship for anyone.

Her mother snitched another fry. "I'm sure you'll find something suitable soon."

Everything she'd seen had been imminently suitable. Sufficient for her needs. But none were as perfect as the old Whitaker building.

Frowning, she straightened. Pining after the impossible would get her nowhere, much less office space for her business. She needed to get her head out of Laurel Grove and onto reality. Including not moping about Rob and Sophie.

"You're doing exciting work, Juliet."

"My role at Paw Pals has become administrative." She fiddled with the straw in her milkshake. "I miss the interaction with patients. Especially the children. Although without Moose, I suppose it's just as well."

Time hadn't begun to heal the wound in her heart at the loss of her furry friend, either.

She'd assigned several of the newly hired handlers to assume her duties at the hospital. A temporary measure, yet one week had become two. Rolling into three, and still she put off finding a new canine companion for herself.

The condo, her sanctuary, had gone quiet. Too silent without Moose's merry presence. Moose wasn't easily replaced in her heart.

Not any old dog would do. It took an exceptional, responsive and empathetic animal to be fit for the work at Paw Pals.

"I saw Moose yesterday."

Sometimes it was like her mother could read her mind. "You did? Where? What was he doing? How is he?"

"Moose was his usual perky self." Her mom stuffed the remains of her lunch into the white takeout bag. "He and Sophie stopped by the Ewe yesterday morning with Evelyn."

Her heart turned over. "And Sophie? How is she?"

"She's doing well. Thanks to you. Laughing, happy. Her old, bubbly self." Her mother rested her elbows on the table. The silver bangles on her wrists clanked and jangled. "The three of them were on their way to the library for story time. Moose has become a beloved, literary pooch pal."

Juliet blinked back her tears. Everything she'd hoped for Sophie. She'd been right to leave Moose with her.

She desperately wanted to ask her mom about Rob, but she couldn't bring herself to say the words.

They deposited their trash in the bin and got into Juliet's car. Her mother maintained a steady stream of chatter, updating her on the latest Laurel Grove goings-on.

Part of her was desperate for news of Rob. Another part wasn't sure she could handle the mere mention of his name without dissolving into a puddle of tears.

She steered into the medical office parking lot to an empty space beside her mom's car. "Are you headed home?"

Her mother shook her head. "I need to deliver the Knit-Knack Club's latest project, Hats 4 Hope, to the neonatal unit."

Juliet turned off the engine and, with a click, released her seat belt. "Let me help you carry the box."

"I've got it. I'm sure you have lots of Paw Pals stuff to take care of."

Actually, not so much. She'd been working like a crazed person over the last few weeks. Anything to keep from brooding over Rob.

Her mother started to release her seat belt and then sat back. "Oh, I nearly forgot to tell you the biggest news."

She fumbled in her purse. "Rob was honored by the Greensboro PD and the mayor for his heroic actions in apprehending the shooter and saving lives."

Juliet's shoulders hitched.

"It was quite the occasion at City Hall with the other survivors there as well." Her mom drew her cell out of her bag. "Evelyn sent me several photos."

Dragging her finger across the screen, her mom held it for Juliet to see. "Doesn't Sophie look sweet in her dress?"

It was the frilly pink dress with the cap sleeves and filmy chiffon overskirt that they'd bought together. The dress Sophie said made her look so bee-you-ti-ful. Juliet found it hard to breathe.

With her thumb and forefinger, her mom enlarged the photo. She held it for Juliet to take a closer look. "Everyone got dressed in their finest for the ceremony."

Juliet spotted Evelyn in a lacy blue dress that matched her Melbourne blue eyes. Looking impossibly handsome in a suit and tie, Rob stood next to his aunt. Her heart did a somersault. He cleaned up nice. So very, very nice.

Her mother swiped to another photo, pointing out the small dog at Sophie's feet. "Moose was looking debonair, too."

Juliet smiled at her furry, well-groomed friend, sporting a black-striped bowtie. The matching leash looped over Rob's arm.

But she did a double take when she spotted the woman standing on the other side of Rob. A gorgeous blonde with a radiant smile. Rob's arm draped casually across her shoulders.

"Rob has other reasons to celebrate." Her mother smiled brightly. "But it's his news to tell."

Sucker punched, she felt as if the oxygen left her lungs in one fell swoop.

Despite his declaration of love, he'd wasted no time in replacing her in his affections. But hurt outweighed any spark of anger she might have felt.

Her mom took back her phone. "Such a lovely family photograph."

Family? Is that what Rob, Sophie, Moose and the unknown woman were? A family?

But why shouldn't they be a family? She'd had her chance and thrown it away. He'd moved on. He'd found someone.

He deserved someone wonderful in his life. Sophie needed a mother. Yet the idea of someone else being Sophie's mom made Juliet feel queasy.

As for the ache in her heart for Rob… It was a chasm so big she couldn't begin to wrap her mind around the pain.

"Is everything okay, Juliet?" Her mom slung the purse strap over her arm. "You look pale all of a sudden."

She made a conscious effort to breathe. "Just tired, I guess."

Her mother cupped her cheek in her palm. "Try not to overdo it, darling. Paw Pals won't be built in a day, or even a month."

She gave her mom a quick hug and released her. "I'll try."

Her mother opened the car door. "Are you headed to the hospital?"

At the moment, she could think of nothing worse than facing colleagues. The way this day was going, she'd probably run into the CEO and humiliate herself by bursting into tears.

She swallowed. "I think I'll work from home this afternoon."

Her mom got out of the car. "I enjoyed lunch."

She made an attempt to pull her scattered emotions together. "I did, too. Text me when you get home so I'll know you're safe."

"Will do. Love you," her mother called.

"Love you, too. Talk to you soon."

Her head throbbed, but it was nothing compared to the pain in her heart.

Chapter Fourteen

Almost on autopilot, Juliet drove to her apartment.
Moose and Sophie. Rob and the woman. The images
played in an unending loop through her head.

Grabbing her work bag, she fled to the safety of her
condo.

Once inside, she gave up the pretense of holding it together. Dropping the briefcase, a sob tore from her throat.
Her back to the wall, she slid to the floor.

Moose. Sophie. Rob. Josh.

Every one of them lost to her. Her gaze skittered to
her wedding portrait on the mantel. Lancing pain stabbed
at her chest.

Hair falling into her face, she curled into a ball. Tor-
tured sobs racked her body. Stealing her breath. Goug-
ing her heart.

Juliet cried as she hadn't cried since the two Marines
rang her doorbell in Jacksonville. She cried for what had
been and would never be again. She sobbed until she had
no tears left to cry.

No matter how hard she tried to hold on to Josh and to
what they'd been to each other, the finality of his death

overcame her in a way she hadn't been willing to face before. Life went on. Life must always go on.

And in that bitter, painful realization, for the first time in five years, she came to terms with the inescapable fact that her life must move forward.

Josh was gone. And nothing she could ever do would bring him back, or that golden time she'd had with him.

The day she lost him, she also lost the girl she'd been with Josh. Without him, without an anchor, she'd been adrift ever since. Trying to find her way back to that girl.

Her body shuddered with a hiccuped breath. Heartbreak had changed her. She was a different person now.

With Rob and Sophie, she'd glimpsed a way back to the bits and pieces that remained of that girl. More than that, she'd seen a way for the two parts of herself to at last become one. She'd liked the person she'd been in the process of becoming with them.

It felt like she'd been in that process for a long, long time. In a kind of liminal zone. Like a marsh bird stuck in the mud, caught between the sea and terra firma.

Trapped in a cocoon of her own making. She inhaled sharply. Just as Rob had said.

And suddenly more than anything—more than she wanted even Rob and Sophie—she wanted to simply be free.

Free of the weight of bereavement. Free to embrace the joys of life again.

She squeezed her eyelids shut. "Please help me, Lord," she whispered. "I'm so sorry I shut you out."

With hindsight's clarity, she realized God had been there all along. Suffering with her through the sorrow. Juliet truly beheld His heart for her. Her mom had said it best—a parent could only be as happy as His saddest child.

"I'm so weary of struggling with this pain. Please, help me to be brave enough to move on from here," she whispered.

But how? Outside the window, a bird chirped. She pushed the hair out of her face. An idea slowly filtered through her brain.

Her heart constricted. There must be another way. An easier way.

Rob told her once grief takes as long as it takes. And with a gut-twisting wrench deep inside her, she knew—*she knew*—it was finally time to say goodbye and let Josh go.

Fifteen minutes later, she arrived at the cemetery. She entered through the small iron gate and followed a well-trod path to his grave. Stuck in the ground beside the headstone, a small American flag fluttered. She lay her hand atop the cool granite.

> *Joshua Tyler Newkirk*
> *Captain U.S. Marine Corps*
> *Afghanistan*
> *March 20, 1989-August 31, 2017*
> *Beloved husband*
> *Semper Fidelis*

Over the years, she'd gotten into the habit of bringing flowers every week. The last time she was here had been the day she went to Laurel Grove to take the Melbourne case. The flowers she'd left in the vase had long since withered.

She removed the dried-up stems. This time, she'd brought nothing to replace them.

Only herself.

She sank into grass. "Hello, my darling."

Josh would have wanted so much more for her than the empty future she'd relegated to herself over the last five years.

Captain Joshua Newkirk had lived and died with courage. As his widow, she must do no less than to live out her days with courage, too. Anything else would dishonor what they'd been to each other.

"I love you so much, Josh," she whispered.

For a moment, she blocked out everything else but him.

The twinkle in his eyes. The playful laughter they'd shared. The heartrending quirk of his smile when they'd danced at their wedding.

She relived all of it. One last time. Just her and him.

Like a caress, the summer breeze lifted a strand of her hair and gently feathered it across her cheek. She took a deep, cleansing breath.

Juliet recalled Rob's words to Sophie that last morning. True for her as well.

"Sometimes we have to say goodbye. Whether we want to or not." Her voice broke. "Wh-whether we're ready to or not."

Juliet gazed through the dappled shade into the blue Carolina sky. "I'll never forget you, Josh, but I have to let you go."

She saw now that in making room in her heart for someone new, she didn't have to lose her memories of him. Because what was most important about the people she loved, she got to keep, to treasure. For always.

This transformation within herself had come too late for her and Rob. She'd hurt him too much. But God would be there for her through it all.

"I won't be coming back here for a long time, Josh. But that's okay." She sighed. "I'm okay."

Or at least, with God's help she would be. Josh wasn't here. He'd found a truer home than the one they'd shared. Time for her to make a new home—a new life—for herself.

A black-and-yellow swallowtail butterfly glided to a perch atop the headstone. Tears stung her eyelids. Its loveliness was breathtaking.

And somehow she knew this creature was a gift to her. A gift from a good, good Father.

"Thank You, Lord."

A peace unlike anything she'd ever known descended upon her. The chains binding her to her grief-stricken misery lifted. No longer weighing her down. She was free.

Then, with a swift flicker of its wings, the butterfly lifted from the granite and flitted upward. Flying free. Catching the wind. Soaring higher and higher until it disappeared into a grove of trees.

"Goodbye, my darling." She took one last look at the gravestone. "Semper fidelis, Josh. Semper fidelis."

Always faithful. Like her Father God. To the very end.

She stood up. It was time to forge a new beginning. To find her way home.

When he got the text from Lesley Mitchell asking him to come over that afternoon for an update on Juliet, he left the Laurel Grove police station in the capable hands of his second-in-command.

Each morning, the first thing he thought about was Juliet. She was also the last thing he thought about when he closed his eyes at night. Every minute in between was like a physical ache.

Why had he believed letting her go to miss him was a good idea? What had he been thinking? She'd returned to her life with not so much as a backward glance.

He found it impossible to concentrate. Not ideal, considering he was in the midst of settling into his new job as Laurel Grove's newest chief of police.

At the old Victorian, he spotted Lesley in one of the white wicker rockers grouped in a cluster at the end of the turreted porch. The heady scent of gardenias wafted through the air.

Rob hugged her. "Aunt Evie tells me your doctor visit went well today. How was Juliet?"

Her mom motioned him into an adjacent chair. "She seemed off, though I couldn't put my finger on why."

"She's probably tired from getting Paw Pals up and running."

Lesley shook her head. "It was more than that. Although, I could tell she's struggling with not having her own dog."

"I'm working on that. I'm going to see a potential candidate later this week. Still wondering about how and when to approach Juliet about this. I'm nervous about how she might respond."

The silver bracelets on Lesley's arms gleamed in the late afternoon sunshine. "Juliet's going to be ecstatic at the prospect of a new canine friend."

"I hope so."

He'd had his doubts. Especially lying awake in the middle of the night, staring at the darkened ceiling. Considering the many ways his gift could go wrong. And blow up in his face.

"The last thing I want is to guilt her into something she's not ready for, or make her feel pressured." He gripped the chair. "That's why I've kept my distance. This is my gift to her. No strings attached."

"Which is one of the reasons I love you, Rob. For how well you love her and want the best for her, even at your own expense." Lesley squeezed his arm. "When I think about the sacrifices you've made—"

He shook his head. "It's not a sacrifice when you love someone. Especially if it makes her feel safe, Miss Lesley."

Juliet's mother smiled. "You have respected her misguided wishes, but in this situation 'love me, love my dog' totally speaks her language."

He cocked his head. "Did she ask after me?"

"No…but I can tell she misses you."

"Maybe she misses Sophie and Moose, but not me." He blew out a breath. "I'm not sure absence is making her heart grow fonder. Maybe my approach has been wrong all along."

He hadn't heard from her since she left Laurel Grove. Three weeks, two days and ten hours to be exact. Not that he was counting.

"I'm not easily discouraged, but this biding my time to let her miss me doesn't seem to be working the way I intended." He scoured his face with his hand. "There's only been a deafening silence."

He'd felt edgy and off-balance ever since she went away.

"Am I fooling myself? Maybe she'll never love me the way I love her."

"Don't give up on her, Rob." Lesley pushed up her glasses with the tip of her finger. "I believe she's finally coming to terms with Josh's death."

He sat forward. "What did she say?"

"It wasn't so much what she said as what she didn't

say." Lesley settled into her chair. "I was showing her the photos from the award ceremony. Come to think of it, that's when she went quiet."

He gazed over the tree-shaded street. "It's just hard. Waiting for her to decide whether she wants a life with me and Sophie."

"I got the distinct impression she was upset, but trying hard not to show it." Lesley patted his hand. "Thank you for being so patient with my daughter."

"What else can I do?" He rose. "I love her." His throat closed with emotion.

"Hang in there, darling." She gave him a quick hug. "Like I told Juliet this morning, the best things are worth the wait. Please give Sophie and Moose my love."

On the drive home, he considered his next step in the effort to win Juliet's heart.

He'd never been the type of guy to sit around waiting for life to happen. Almost from the moment she drove away, he'd begun visiting rescue shelters for a suitable therapy dog substitute for Juliet's beloved Moose.

No one could replace what Moose had meant to her following the death of her husband. But he'd never met a more caring, nurturing woman. She loved with every fiber of her being. Her work through Paw Pals was so significant.

He never wanted her to lose that. Any dog would be blessed to be the recipient of such devotion. As would any child privileged to call her mother.

As for the man who'd get to call her wife? He rubbed the back of his neck.

He'd been so sure she'd soon return to Laurel Grove. To him and Sophie.

Three weeks, two days and ten-plus hours later, he

was less sure. Increasingly beset by lingering fears she was lost to him forever.

"Please, God," he whispered. "Even if I'm not meant to be in her life, for her sake, let this be the right dog."

A disquieting feeling had been building in his gut. His conversation with Lesley had only reinforced that the time to act was now.

Bright and early tomorrow, he, Sophie and Moose were taking a road trip to see a man about a dog. And then, they'd pay a visit to a certain beautiful therapy dog handler in Greensboro.

Over the next several days, Juliet thought about what she wanted the rest of her life to look like. About what was most important to her.

After that, it was only a matter of making the necessary adjustments to accommodate her new priorities.

Juliet wanted to move back to her hometown to be closer to her mom. She'd miss her friends in Greensboro, but Laurel Grove wasn't that far. The slower pace of small-town life suited her.

She also wasn't yet ready to let go of her dreams of a life with Rob and Sophie. She'd hurt him. Perhaps done irreparable damage to any future they could ever have together.

There was the added wrinkle of the new woman in his life. But she had nothing to lose from trying and potentially everything to gain.

In his own words, all was fair in love and war. Well, she'd decided to bring the war for his love to his doorstep.

She was prepared to do anything in her power to win back her place in his life. She'd beg his forgiveness. Find a way to earn back his faith in her. Prove to him she could be trusted to not hurt him or Sophie again if he'd give her another chance.

Yet if her relationship with Rob didn't work out as she hoped and prayed, relocating to Laurel Grove would mean she'd have an up close and excruciating proximity to Sophie being mothered by someone else.

But the tenacious, mission-oriented overachiever Rob remembered from high school hadn't completely disappeared. She couldn't live with herself if she didn't tell him how she felt. Then, the choice would be his.

First on her list—she signed a contract to lease-to-own the old Whitaker building. Second—she hired a contractor to renovate the space into Paw Pals headquarters. Third—she listed her Greensboro condo with a real estate agent.

In this market, the agent warned her she could have an offer by the weekend.

The sooner, the better.

Ending the call to the agent, Juliet bit her lip. Her mom would let her camp out with her until she found her own house in Laurel Grove. Preferably one that came with an adorable four-year-old girl and her irresistible father.

The next item on her agenda—she joined the Grief-Share group at a local church. Something she should have done five years ago. God never meant for His children to walk through life's difficulties alone. That's why He'd given them each other.

She spent Friday morning packing up the contents of her kitchen cabinets. She'd acquired very little in the way of personal possessions over the five years of her life here. Amazing and sad.

Having emptied the last cabinet under the sink, she eased onto the heels of her sneakers. Using her forearm, she swiped at her brow. She'd been treading water for too long. Time to head for the deep end.

What was the saying about going big or going—

On the counter, her cell buzzed.

She caught hold of the corner as she sought to disentangle her feet out from under her. Sitting on her haunches for so long, her legs had gone to sleep.

Lurching into the counter, she made a grab for the phone. "Hello?" she gasped.

"Juliet. It's Rob."

The bottom of her stomach dropped to her toes. And she found herself having more than a little difficulty filling her lungs with oxygen.

"Hi," she squeaked.

She cringed. Could she sound more idiotic?

"Are you all right?"

"What do you mean?" she rasped.

"You sound out of breath. Did I catch you at a bad time?"

"Sorry. No. I was busy, you see. And I was on the floor. And my feet got tangled." She was babbling, but she couldn't stop herself.

Like she was still a tongue-tied seventeen-year-old in the presence of the swoon-inducing Rob Melbourne.

"And…and I was cleaning…"

"Is everything okay, Juliet?"

"Of course. I'm fine. Everything's fine."

Stupid. Nothing was fine. Tell him how you really are. How you die a little bit every day you're apart from him.

"Good." A second of silence followed. "I'm glad to hear you're doing well."

She wasn't doing well. She was doing awful. Why was it so hard to tell him how she felt? She squeezed her eyes shut.

Leaning her elbow on the countertop, she rested her

forehead in her hand. Why did she become such an idiot around him?

"I wasn't sure you'd answer…" His voice thickened.

Her eyes snapped open. Was it her imagination, or did Rob sound nervous?

"…when you recognized my number."

"I didn't get a chance to look at caller ID before I answered." She winced as the words came out of her mouth. That's not what she'd meant at all.

"Oh." His voice dropped a notch.

"But I would've picked up anyway. Even if I'd known it was you."

Making it sound like he was the last person she wanted to talk to? The truth was the exact opposite.

Stop talking, Juliet. Just stop talking.

"I'm sorry to bother you when you're…busy."

She sighed. "Can we start this conversation over again? Hi, Rob. I tripped over my clumsy feet in my haste to answer the phone. I was doing the exciting, glamorous work of cleaning out the cabinet underneath my sink. I'm delighted to hear from you. I'm so glad you called. How are you?"

This time he laughed. Rich, warm. Genuine. Like the Rob she'd come to know—and love.

Yes, she was ready to admit she loved him. If only she could get the words around the clumsy foot stuck in her mouth.

"I'm good, Juliet. Better now that I'm talking to you." His voice hoarsened, happily curling her toes.

She sank into the nearest kitchen chair, lest her knees buckle and send her crashing once more to the linoleum. "Me, too."

"Listen, I was wondering if you were free tomorrow afternoon. Sophie has really missed you…"

But what about you, Rob? Have you missed me? Tell him how you feel.

Her courage failed her. "I… I've missed her, too."

"I hoped maybe I could bring her and Moose to Greensboro to visit you?"

Her heart leaped at the prospect of seeing two of the people she loved most. Even if he was only doing it for his daughter, she'd take what she could get.

"I'd love that, Rob."

"Great."

She could hear the smile in his voice.

"I was thinking around two o'clock. How about we meet at the carousel near the science center?"

She clutched the phone to her ear. "That sounds perfect."

"You girls can visit for an hour or so before I pick her up again."

She frowned. "You won't be joining us?"

"I can't stay. I have a few important errands to run."

"Oh." Disappointment dropped like a lead ball in her chest. "I was hoping to get a chance to talk."

"When I come back for Sophie, we can catch up then."

"I… I have some news." Clearing her throat, she screwed up her courage. "That I hope will please you."

"Let's save it for tomorrow, okay? I have some news of my own. I made everyone from Laurel Grove keep it under wraps. I wanted you to hear it from me first."

Nausea roiled her belly. So it was true. He was coming to tell her he was in love with the blonde woman. Her heart shattered.

"Until tomorrow, Juliet."

"Until then," she whispered.

As soon as he clicked off, she laid her head on the table and cried.

She'd waited too long. She'd lost him for good.

Chapter Fifteen

Heartsore, Juliet arrived early enough the next afternoon to park and amble over to where the historic carousel held court just beyond the Greensboro Science Center.

Nearly sick with anxiety, she sank onto a nearby bench to watch for them. The recreational complex was busy with families out for a day of fun. The aroma of fresh-cut grass filled the air.

Spotting the familiar charcoal-gray pickup pull into the parking lot, she straightened. When Rob and Sophie got out of the truck, her heart fluttered. Bracing for his news, she focused on Sophie. In a navy and yellow flower short set, the little girl looked so sweet.

Crossing over, Moose barked. His tail went into the rapid-fire swish-swish he did when he was happy.

Reaching the curb, Sophie waved. "Miss Juliet!" The child ran straight into her arms.

And she forgot about everything, except for loving Sophie.

Tears blurred Juliet's vision. "I missed you so much," she said into the child's silky soft hair.

Sophie lifted her head, her big blue eyes wide. "I missed you, too."

Yipping, Moose rubbed against them, clearly wishing to get in on the action. Juliet let go of Sophie long enough to shower the small dog with some love of his own.

Rob folded his arms across the blue shirt that matched his eyes. "Hi, Juliet."

Juliet looked at him. "Hello, Rob." She rose. But her knees and her nerve threatened to quit on her.

Sophie wrapped herself around Juliet, clinging to her side. And Juliet wasn't sure just who was supporting whom.

Completely unaware of the effect he had on the entire female population, Juliet in particular, he just smiled. "It's good to see you."

She swallowed and reminded herself to breathe.

He pulled his phone from his cargo shorts and glanced at it. "How about we check back with you ladies in about an hour?"

We?

From the passenger side of his truck, fair hair gleamed in the sunlight. Her heart stopped. Was Rob really going to introduce her to his new lady friend at Country Park in Greensboro?

He half turned. "Oh, I nearly forgot. You said you had news?"

Be as brave as Sophie...

She raised her chin. "I've decided to make Laurel Grove the headquarters for Paw Pals."

His gaze sharpened. "You're buying the Whitaker building?"

She kept her arm around Sophie's shoulders. "I am."

"Does this mean you...?" His gaze sharpened.

"I'm moving back to Laurel Grove."

Something eased in his expression. "That is good news."

"I hoped you'd think so." She steeled herself. "And your news?"

"There's someone I want you to meet."

She held herself rigidly erect. "I wish the best for you and Sophie."

"Okay…" He gave her a curious look. "Thanks?"

Sophie pulled at her. "Can we ride the carousel now?" The little girl bounced. "And rent a swan boat? And get a snow cone?"

Her dad frowned. "Sophie!"

Juliet laughed. "Of course, we can. Every single one of those things."

He pulled out his wallet.

She shook her head. "Absolutely not. I'm going to enjoy this as much as Sophie. I've got this."

"It's girl time." Sophie arched her brow. "Bye, Daddy."

He rolled his eyes. "Well, I know when I've been dismissed. Thrown over for a snow cone, no less."

Despite the quaking of her knees, Juliet managed to flutter her lashes at him. "Snow cone today. Boyfriend before you know it."

Clutching his chest, he staggered. "Don't remind me." But he laughed.

Juliet's heart skipped a beat. How she'd missed this easy camaraderie. And the sheer pleasure of simply being with him. If he'd give her the chance to love him, she'd never take his love for granted again.

He gave his daughter a quick peck on the cheek, but Sophie tugged at Juliet's hand.

She had only time to call out an abrupt goodbye before Sophie hauled her down the steps to the pedal boats on the lake. On his leash, Moose scampered ahead of them.

With the tiny dog perched on the seat between them like a fluffy canine masthead, they pedaled around the small lake in a pink swan boat. Afterward, they found a shady spot under one of the trees to eat the shaved ice slo-ball.

Sophie stuck out her tongue. "Am I purple?"

Juliet winked. "As a grape." She hadn't gotten one for herself.

But she fed Moose plain shaved ice. Without any syrup that might contain additives harmful to her furry friend.

She and her favorite little girl laughed and talked as hard as they could. Before Juliet knew it, it was time for Rob to return.

They climbed the steps above the lake to the plaza above. Rob was already there, waiting for them outside the octagonal structure that housed the carousel.

Alone.

Juliet released a breath.

Sophie planted her hands on her tiny hips. "We didn't ride the carousel yet, Daddy."

Juliet hugged the child close. "Moose wouldn't have been allowed to ride anyway."

"I could still ride." She puffed out her chest. "I'm big enough to ride by myself now."

"Not today. Remember our plan." He put his hand on his daughter's shoulder. "It's time to say goodbye, Soph."

Already? Her heart sank. Their time together hadn't been enough.

Goodbye meant goodbye to Sophie's dad, too. Her talk with Rob wasn't happening. Disappointment swirled in her chest.

The little girl perked. "We're getting cheese pizza at DiPalma's for dinner, but another one with green peppers for Uncle Adrian." She made a face. "Yuck."

She crouched beside the child and hugged her. "It was so wonderful to see you."

Taking Moose's small face in her hand, she planted a kiss on his furry head. "Take good care of my Sophie, dear friend."

Sophie laughed. "We take care of each other. Bye, Miss Juliet." She pulled away from Juliet, leaving her arms empty.

Rob kept a firm grip on his child. "Hang on there, Soph."

"Thanks for this afternoon, Rob."

Suddenly, she didn't know what to do with her hands. She dared not touch him, much less embrace him, or she'd be lost.

"You don't know how much it has meant to me. Have a safe trip to Laurel Grove." She willed her heart to steady and the tears building behind her eyelids not to fall. "Goodbye," she whispered.

"Uh… If it's okay with you, I'd like to stay a little longer to talk. Aunt Evie is going to take Sophie home." He motioned to someone in the parking lot.

Juliet spotted Evelyn getting out of Rob's truck. Had it been Evelyn's silvery hair she'd seen earlier?

"But I thought…" She bit her lip.

"You thought what?"

Once Evelyn reached the curb, Rob released Sophie, who hustled over to her great-aunt.

Juliet cocked her head. "If Miss Evelyn is driving your truck, how will you get home?"

A familiar red truck pulled alongside Evelyn and Sophie. Leaning across the seat, Adrian waved through the open window. Evelyn and Sophie got into his vehicle.

Rob's shoulders relaxed a notch. "The logistics have been slightly complicated in putting together this surprise for you."

"You wanted me to meet someone?"

He gave her a bright smile. "Oh, that's still to come."

Right. The new girlfriend. She could do without that kind of surprise.

But she wanted the chance to talk to him, and she'd take any time she could get. *Stop stalling. Courage…*

She squared her shoulders. "Rob, I wanted to… I need to—"

"Would you mind if we walk while we talk?"

Juliet shrugged. "Sure?" What else could she say?

Sometimes it was easier to talk when engaged in something physical. And Rob was a physical kind of guy.

"Where should we walk?"

He gestured to the trees behind the science center. "I was thinking we could take the trail over to the cannon."

The forested walking paths were popular with joggers and cyclists. Country Park sat adjacent to the greenway that looped around the site of the Battle of Guilford Courthouse, Greensboro's American Revolution claim to fame.

Underneath the dappled shade cast by the large, towering oaks and hickory trees, they strolled, side by side, in silence for a few minutes. A peaceful place, belying the conflict that occurred here two hundred and forty years ago.

She'd recently fought her own struggle for freedom. Nothing ventured, nothing gained. "I owe you an apology."

He faltered, but quickly recovered his step. "You don't owe me anything, Juliet." He kept his face toward the trail.

"I owe you an apology and an explanation. I wasn't truthful with you that last day in Laurel Grove." She swallowed. "Because I wasn't being truthful with myself."

As they walked, he kept his head down. Making it difficult to read his expression.

She touched his arm. "Rob?"

"Before you say anything, there's several things I need to tell you. I've made a big change in my life." He faced her. "The shooting clarified something I'd been thinking about for a long time. Something I needed to do for Sophie's sake. Sophie understands my reasons, and she's on board. It's been a change, but a good one. I…"

He continued to talk but she stopped listening, unable to hear him for the pounding of her heart. Too late. She'd left this too late. She'd lost him.

For Sophie's sake. He'd fallen in love with someone else. Juliet closed her eyes.

"…so that's why I'm the new police chief in Laurel Grove."

Her eyes flew open. "What did you say?"

Rob frowned. "Which part? Vernon letting me know the old chief was retiring? Or me quitting my job as a detective with the Greensboro PD?"

Juliet was speechless.

"So…what do you think?" He jammed his hands in his pockets, shuffling his feet. As if he were nervous about her reaction. As if her response mattered.

Hope took a sudden leap toward life. "This is your big change? This is your news everyone's been hinting about?"

"Well… Yeah." He furrowed his brow. "What did you think I was talking about?"

Her runaway imagination had taken him to the altar with a veritable trio of potential brides—the school-teacher, the pharmacist, Dr. Erickson.

"Juliet?"

Snapping back to reality, she gave him a tremulous smile. "Yes?"

"What do you think of my career change?" He hunched his shoulders. "Unless you're not interested in my life."

She almost laughed. Since the age of seventeen, she'd been the exact opposite of uninterested.

"It means a regular nine-to-five workday at the station, unless there's a sudden, unprecedented Laurel Grove crime wave. Mostly, it's an administrative job. Less danger. More time for loved ones." He wore a hurt look. "I hoped you'd be pleased."

"Oh, Rob. I am pleased for you and Sophie." She laced her hands together. "I'm sorry for being distracted. I think Laurel Grove just scored the best new police chief in the state. But there's something I've been dying to tell—"

His cell dinged. "Just a sec." He glanced at a message on the screen and held up his index finger. "Hold that thought."

This was getting ridiculous. Was he ever going to give her the chance to tell him she loved him?

"Next surprise." He smiled. "The someone I want you to meet has arrived."

In her relief over discovering he'd taken a new job, not a new woman, into his life, she'd hoped the surprises were at an end.

Taking a giant sidestep off the trail, she sank onto a nearby bench.

He grinned. "I'll bring her to you."

She could only stare at him, mute. Her head throbbed. She felt sick to her stomach. This couldn't be happening. *Where are You, God? Help me. Please.*

Taking long strides, he returned to the path and soon disappeared from over the next rise in the hilly footpath.

She spent the next few minutes trying not to hyperventilate. Breathe in… Breathe out… She put her hand to her chest.

A silver-haired gentleman appeared at the top of the incline with Rob. She squinted. From a distance, he resembled Rob's uncle. But it couldn't be. Where were Evelyn and Sophie?

On the end of the leash in Rob's hand, a puppy barked. With a wave, Adrian headed away. Rob and the small golden retriever started toward her.

What in the world? "Rob?"

Straining forward, the puppy gave an excited yip and licked her ankle.

Rob grimaced. "Sorry about that. She hasn't gone through her Canine Good Citizen training yet. But she's smart, a real people pleaser and all those other traits that make for a great therapy dog."

"I'm sorry. What?"

"An old Raleigh PD buddy of mine, who's now a police chief in a small town in the Blue Ridge, has been helping me look. It's taken us nearly a month to find the right match."

"Just to be clear." She frowned at him. "We're talking about your match with a dog?"

"No…" He handed her the leash. "*Your* match with a dog."

Unable to resist the adorable fluff ball at her feet, she scooped her onto the bench. The puppy promptly laid her head on Juliet's lap. She laughed.

Rob grinned. "She's perfect. Sophie's already in love with her."

Juliet stroked the little dog behind the ears. The puppy made a happy, whining noise. Her heart melted. She'd missed having a canine companion. "What's her name?"

"That's up to you. She's nine weeks old. I figured it

was best to get her young so you could train her right from the start."

"She's for me?" She peered at him. "I don't understand."

Rob sat down with the puppy between them. "You told me a dog picks his person. Moose loves Soph, that's for sure. But he misses you, Jules. Every evening before he curls up in his doggie bed, he goes from room to room. I think he's looking for you."

Her heart constricted.

"I couldn't stand the idea of you missing him as much as he missed you." Rob gave her a crooked smile. "We all miss you. More than you can possibly imagine."

Her heart thudded.

"I've missed you and Sophie, too," she rasped. "More than you can possibly imagine."

"You don't know how happy it makes me to hear you say that. I've wondered if I was doing the right thing…" He looked away.

"So you got me a dog?"

"You've done so much for us. I wanted to give you back your calling by giving you a dog. Let me do this for you, Jules."

The puppy snuggled against her.

"For the record, Moose and the puppy get along great." Rob stuck his tongue in his cheek. "Although she's twice his size, there's no question Moose is the boss."

"Little dog, big attitude," she chuckled.

"Sophie and I have come up with a few options we'd like you to consider."

"I'm listening."

"Golden retrievers are naturally friendly, intelligent and devoted." He gave her the self deprecating grin that melted her insides. "Kind of like me. The puppy is yours.

Or Moose comes back to you. The puppy becomes Sophie's, but with you moving to Laurel Grove we'd love if you'd consider helping Sophie train her to become a therapy dog."

"Sophie wants me to have Moose?"

"Moose wants you, Juliet." Dropping his gaze, he rubbed the puppy's back. "As do I, but I understand your fears about loving and losing. If you can't let the puppy into your heart, Soph and I will take her."

Her fingers found his. "If I may, I'd like to propose a third option."

Rob's head lifted.

No longer wanting there to be any space between them, she placed the puppy in her lap. Settling in, the little dog went to sleep.

Juliet told Rob about visiting Josh's grave. About making her peace with his death and with God.

"I love you, Rob." Her voice caught. "You're all I think about—morning, noon and night. There's room in my heart for Moose, the puppy, Sophie…and you. Most of all, you. If you'll have me."

He scanned her features. "I meant what I said about not being good at goodbyes, Juliet. That day, I let you go because I felt God was not done with either of us."

She stilled. "I'm sorry for hurting you. God used your words to bring me to the point I could let go of the grief. Please tell me you haven't stopped loving me."

He gripped her hand. "I could never stop loving you, Juliet."

In his eyes, she beheld his heart. And in his heart, home.

A gratitude so deep, so true, surged through her being. He loved her. Rob still loved her.

Juliet touched his hair. His face. His mouth. She'd

never get enough of being able to touch him. To love him. With her whole heart.

He kissed the inside of her hand.

"You were right, my darling." She cradled his cheek. "In this life, there's tragedy and heartbreak, but also beauty and joy. I love you, Rob. So, so much."

His eyes—those beautiful, electrifying eyes of his—lit up.

"I'm so ready to discover that joy with you." Her breath hitched. "I'm just sorry it took me so long to get here."

"You don't ever have to apologize about your feelings for Josh." Tipping up her chin, his gaze locked into hers. "You grieved deeply, because you love deeply."

A tear rolled down her face.

"Don't cry, sweetheart." He caught her teardrop on the tip of his finger. "You know I can't stand to see you cry."

"For the brightness of tomorrow." She inhaled softly. "Here's to tomorrow."

"To as many tomorrows as the Lord allows."

This good, good man must never be allowed to doubt the depth of her love.

"My love for you is as vast as the sky…" Her mouth trembled. "And as near as my beating heart."

He leaned forward and kissed her. His kiss held the bittersweet remembrance of what each of them had lost and would never forget. But it also held the tantalizing promise of what lay ahead. For the family—for the children—they would create together.

Each day the Lord gave them was a precious gift. Their love for each other was the gift they gave to Him.

Epilogue

Juliet closed the door softly behind her. From his favorite perch on the ottoman, Moose lifted his head as she tiptoed into the living room.

"It won't be long now," she told him.

Her gaze cut to the clock. It was almost time for Rob and Sophie to get home. What a difference a year made.

Headed to the kitchen to put the finishing touches on dinner, she couldn't help stopping by the picture on the mantel of her and Rob on their wedding day. They'd married only a few months after she returned to Laurel Grove.

Remembering that happy day, she touched a finger to the photograph. Surrounded by family and friends, Uncle Adrian had walked her down the aisle of the church. In her frilly pink dress, Sophie had been the most adorable flower girl ever. Satin pillow harnessed to his Paw Pals vest, Moose strutted his stuff as their canine ring bearer.

Tearing herself away, Juliet ventured into the kitchen to check the timer. Headlights swept across the front of the house. As Rob's truck pulled into the driveway, Moose gave a short bark.

"Yes, thank you very much for the heads-up." Wiping her hands on a dish towel, she smiled at her furry companion. She cut her eyes toward the hall. "But let's keep the noise down, shall we? We're living on borrowed time as it is."

Jumping to the floor and tail wagging like a flag in a brisk wind, the tiny dog scampered toward the door. Sophie, clutching Bixby's leash, burst inside.

"Mommy? Guess what?"

If she lived to be a hundred, Juliet reckoned she'd never tire of being Sophie's mom.

Juliet hugged the little bundle of energy, who was close to successfully completing kindergarten. "Tell me."

Moose pranced around them.

"Bixby passed his test." Sophie grinned. "He's now a certified AKC Canine Good Citizen."

Juliet patted the golden retriever's head. "Congratulations, Bixby. Well done."

Bixby licked her hand. The dog had been a sweet addition to their family. Bixby and Moose drifted toward a basket of dog toys.

Rob stepped inside the house. "Hey, sweetheart. Miss me?" A surge of lilac-scented air wafted in after him.

His gaze warmed her. "Always," she whispered. She turned her face up for a kiss. Smiling, he didn't disappoint her.

"You know what this means, right, Mommy?" Sophie unclipped the golden retriever from the leash. "Bix is ready to be a therapy dog at Paw Pals, too. When can we go? Can my baby go, too?" She looked at the empty infant carrier. "Where's Tyler?"

Sophie loved spending time with her new baby brother.

"He's asleep." Juliet shut off the oven timer before it beeped. "Let's hope he stays that way long enough for us to eat a quiet dinner together. The baby might be too little to go just yet, but if Daddy can babysit, you and I could visit the assisted-living facility next weekend."

Rob eased into his recliner. "I never turn down an opportunity to spend time with Tyler. It's a date."

"Great." Sophie bounced over to the table. "When can we eat? I'm starving."

A small cry erupted through the baby monitor.

Juliet sighed. "It would appear you're not the only one."

"I'll get him." Rob rose. "You and Sophie go ahead and sit down."

When Rob didn't immediately return, Juliet got Sophie situated with a few carrot sticks to stave off the worst of the hunger pangs and then went to check on Rob.

She found him in the extra bedroom they'd converted to a nursery. He stood at the rail of the crib, gazing at their two-month-old son.

"Everything okay?" she rasped.

Rob turned his head and smiled. "False alarm. I think he was just dreaming."

When Rob looked at their son like that, Juliet melted every time.

She wrapped her arms around Rob. "Happy dreams, I hope."

"I think so."

She peered around his shoulder. Eyes closed, his lashes soft against his cheeks, the baby's lips turned up sweetly on one corner. A newborn version of his father's irresistible, lopsided smile. Already such a charmer.

Tyler Robert Melbourne. Rob had insisted they give their son Josh's middle name. Her eyes misted, overwhelmed by love, as she gazed at her wonderful husband. Such an exceptional man. Her forever hero.

As if sensing her emotion, Rob pulled her around and kissed her forehead. "Happy?"

Juliet hadn't known she could ever be this happy.

"Very happy." Juliet kissed him again. "I love you."

He held her close in the circle of his arm. With him, she'd found the home of her heart. The only place she ever wanted to find herself. And together they would face all of their tomorrows.

The joys and the tears.

* * * * *

Dear Reader,

There's all kinds of loss.

If you live long enough, you're bound to experience one form or another. Perhaps you've suffered a loss of your own. None is more final than death. Except for the Christ-follower.

Grief is a very personal journey. We grieve deeply because we love deeply. It's the price we pay for love.

Sometimes we have to say goodbye. Whether we want to or not. Whether we're ready to or not. Yet as Juliet discovers, what is most important about the people we love, we get to keep, to treasure. For always.

God never meant for His children to walk through life's difficulties alone. That's why He gave us Himself and each other.

In Rob and Sophie, Juliet finds that the best things in life are absolutely worth the wait. Like the butterflies, we have to be brave, so we don't miss out on the wonderful.

Wherever you find yourself on this road, may God's peace enfold you.

Thank you for sharing Juliet, Rob and Sophie's journey. I pray for you the brightest of tomorrows, full of love, beauty and joy.

I would love to hear from you at lisa@lisacarterauthor.com or visit lisacarterauthor.com.

In His Love,
Lisa Carter

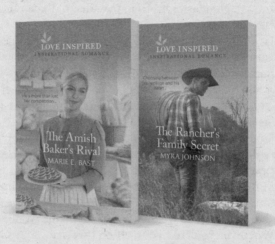

COMING NEXT MONTH FROM
Love Inspired

BUILDING HER AMISH DREAM
Amish of Prince Edward Island • by Jo Ann Brown

Opening a new farm shop on Prince Edward Island is Mattie Albrecht's chance at a fresh start. But avoiding her past becomes impossible when Benjamin Kuhns—her old secret crush—offers to help with repairs. As they work together to renovate the shop, will he restore her heart as well?

THEIR UNPREDICTABLE PATH
by Jocelyn McClay

Despite pressure from his parents, shy widower Jethro Weaver does not want to remarry. And enlisting widow Susannah Mast—a woman ten years his senior—into a fake courtship is just what he needs. But what happens when their fake relationship turns into something real?

THE VETERAN'S VOW
K-9 Companions • by Jill Lynn

Military vet Behr Delgado refuses to participate in a service-dog therapy program, even though it will help with his PTSD. But Ellery Watson is sure she chose the perfect canine companion to improve his life and vows to work with Behr one-on-one. Can they trust each other long enough to heal?

SECRETS OF THEIR PAST
Wander Canyon • by Allie Pleiter

Veterinarian Neal Rodgers lands in Wander Canyon in search of his past. When next-door neighbor Tessa Kennedy begs for his help with a litter of kittens, Neal soon finds himself falling for the sweet small town—and the single mom who might be the key to unlocking the truth...

FATHERHOOD LESSONS
by Gabrielle Meyer

Single dad Knox Taylor is in over his head caring for his twins alone when his nanny leaves unexpectedly. But when their aunt, Merritt Lane, agrees to take care of the children for the summer, Knox might just find the partner he didn't know he was missing.

THE ADOPTION SURPRISE
by Zoey Marie Jackson

After a fatal accident leaves her as guardian to her adopted niece, Kelsey Harris worries about the five-year-old's emotional recovery—until little Morgan meets her long-lost twin, Mia. But as the girls' connection grows, can Kelsey and Mia's widowed adoptive father, Zach Johnson, protect their hearts from the children's matchmaking schemes?

LICNM0122B

SPECIAL EXCERPT FROM

LOVE INSPIRED
INSPIRATIONAL ROMANCE

After a traumatic brain injury, military vet Behr Delgado refuses the one thing that could help him—a service dog. But charity head Ellery Watson knows the dog she selected will improve his quality of life and vows to work with him one-on-one. When their personal lives entwine with their professional lives, can they trust each other long enough to both heal?

Read on for a sneak peek at
The Veteran's Vow *by Jill Lynn!*

Ellery approached and held out Margo's leash for him. She was so excited he was doing better. The thought of disappointing her cut Behr like a combat knife.

Margo stood by Ellery's side, her chocolate face toggling back and forth between them, questioning what she was supposed to do next. Waiting for his lead.

Behr reached out and took the leash. If Ellery noticed his shaking hand, she didn't say anything.

"I want to teach her to stand by your left side. That's it. She's just going to be there. We're going to take it slow." Ellery moved to Behr's left, leaving enough room for Margo to stand between them.

A tremble echoed through him, and Behr tensed his muscles in an effort to curb it.

Margo, on the other hand, would be the first image if someone searched the internet for the definition of the word *calm*.

"Heel." When he gave Margo the command and she obeyed, taking that spot, Behr's heart just about ricocheted out of his chest.

LIEXP0122F

This effort was worth it. Was it, though? He could get through life off-kilter, running into things, tripping, leaving items on the floor when they fell, willing his poor coordination to work instead of using Margo to create balance for him or grasp or retrieve things for him, couldn't he?

Ellery didn't say anything about his audible inhales or exhales, but she had to know what he was up to. The weakness that plagued Behr rose up to ridicule him. It was hard to reveal this side of himself to Ellery, not that she hadn't seen it already. Hard to know that he couldn't just snap his fingers and make his body right again. Hard to remember that he needed this dog and that was why his mom and sisters had signed him up for one.

"You're doing great." Ellery's focus was on Behr, but Margo's tail wagged as if the compliment had been directed at her.

They both laughed, and the tension dissipated like a deployment care package.

"You, too, girl." Ellery offered Margo a treat. "Do you want me to put the balance harness on her so you can feel what it's like?" she asked Behr.

He gave one determined nod.

Ellery strode over to the storage cabinets that lined the back wall. She returned with the harness and knelt to slide it on Margo and adjust it. Behr should probably be watching how to do the same, but right now he was concentrating on standing next to Margo and not having his knees liquefy.

Ellery stood. "See what you think."

Behr gripped the handle, his knuckles turning white. The handle was the right height, and it did make him feel sturdy. Supported.

Like the woman beaming at him from the other side of the dog.

Don't miss
The Veteran's Vow *by Jill Lynn,*
available March 2022 wherever
Love Inspired books and ebooks are sold.

LoveInspired.com

LIEXP0122B